Anonymous

Amalyrac

A Poem

Anonymous

Amalyrac
A Poem

ISBN/EAN: 9783337398026

Printed in Europe, USA, Canada, Australia, Japan

Cover: Foto ©Andreas Hilbeck / pixelio.de

More available books at **www.hansebooks.com**

A M A L Y R A C;

A

P O E M .

Bold and unwavering steps in the difficult pathway of duty,
Trod by a sentinel mind that is ever prepared for the
struggle;
Glances of faith, that follow the Pole star of Heaven's high
calling,
Lead on the militant soul to the Gates of the Temple of
Triumph.

MDCCCLXX.

WISBECH:

PRINTED BY A. BALDING, "MIRROR" OFFICE.

TO

MY BROTHER,

IN REMEMBRANCE

OF MANY

PLEASANT HOURS

SPENT IN

INVESTIGATING THE

"*CHRONICLES OF AMALYRAC.*"

WISBECH, 1857.

CONTENTS.

PRINCIPAL CHARACTERS.

LEONARCHON... ... ... Emperor of Amalyrac.

ARAXES
THERON } ... ... Sons of Leonarchon.
ADONIS

EPIROMENES... ... { Kinsman of the Queen of Epidaurus and General of Amalyrac.

PHILOLAOS ... ... The late Emperor.

HIGH PRIEST OF THE UNKNOWN ... Sovereign Pontiff.

HIGH PRIEST OF THE DAYSTAR.

HIERARCH OF THE WARGOD.

ORONTES or ORO ... ... Favorite of Leonarchon.

ALONZO ... ...Dictator of Islanda.

AMPHILONIN ... ... Chief of Daheo.

LEASCAR ... ... Ruler of Ardoe.

CLEOPATRA ... ... Empress, Wife of Leonarchon.

HERA
CHRYSOTHEMIS } ... ... Daughters of Leonarchon.
IRENE

QUEEN OF EPIDAURUS ... Consort of the late Emperor.

AMARANTHA ... ... Only Child of Philolaos.

PRINTED FOR
PRIVATE CIRCULATION
ONLY.

INTRODUCTION.

Who can check the fleeting Fancy?
Who can bind the grand Ideal?
Who can stay her wings of Swiftness?
Who can curb her steeds of Lightning?
Vain has Reason sought to bind her,
Sought to chain her with his fetters.
Fruitless task! she waves her pinions,
Dewy with etherial splendours,
And with unresisted power,
Soaring upwards, bursts her bondage,
Bursts her chains, and darting onwards,
Leaves behind the far horizon;
Leaves the earth, and in a moment
All around in gleaming order
Sweep the Planets in their courses;
In a moment suns unnumber'd
Roll before in grand procession.
  Onward still, the Pleiad centre
Whirling constellations round it
Stays her not, she leaves its borders
Plunging in the wastes of twilight.
Other stars and other Pleiads,
Rolling vast, round other centres,
Other sunless wastes of darkness—
Other dimly lighted regions—
Spread their endless zones around her.

Onward still ! when lo ! before her
Frowns a dark and awful bulwark ;
High it rears its mighty bastions,
Lost above in clouds of starlight,
Lost beneath in clouds of darkness ;
And the beams of dazzling brightness
That at seasons darted thro' it,
Showed her how it veil'd the glories
Of the Heaven of Heavens behind it.
    Now with bold outstretching pinions,
Up she sweeps with ardent swiftness
Seeking to attain its summit ;
Upward, upward, on she soareth,
Upward thro' the clouds of starlight,
Thro' the hum of universes,
Still it rises up unmeasured—
Still no sign, nor form of ending.
    Then again her wings extended,
Bear her downward, downward, downward,
Downward, thro' the mists of darkness,
Thro' the gleam of mighty systems ;
All in vain she sweepeth onward,
Seeks in vain its vast foundation,
And her wearied pinions failing,
Cease at length to bear her forward,
For upon its front emblazoned
In the dazzling beams of Heaven,
Shone the mystery revealéd,
Shone the name "E T E R N I T Y."
Then she sunk o'erpowered with weakness,
Lost in undefinéd wonder,
And she fell upon the earth-ball,
Fell and fainted into nothing.

Yet she reigns in fairy power,
Reigns supreme upon our planet ;

She can rear the glowing mountain,
She can build the golden palace,
She can spread the emerald garden
Tuneful with the song of streamlets ;
She can bid her helmèd heroes
Fill the astonished world with reverence,
She can bid the great Atlantic
Curb its waves with new-born kingdoms.*
Listen then and hear her wonders,
Listen to a tale of Fancy.

Lo ! she breathed upon the ocean,
Breathed upon the Indian Ocean,
And a land of fairy beauty
Rose above its sunlit billows ;
Lo ! she waves her hand and instant,
Giant mountains raise their summits
Wrapt in everlasting winter ;
All around the peaceful valleys
Lie in verdure neath their shadow
While the floods of mighty rivers
Gleaming in the breadth of sunbeams
Roll their courses to the ocean.
Now she nods and stately kingdoms,
Polish'd nations teem around her,
And the queenly Amalyrac
Rears her lofty towers to Heaven.
See ! she bids the angry tempests
Bear her heroes on their bosom,
Bids the Isles of Elcorada
Nurse them till the time appointed,
Till she leads them on to battle,
Leads them on to deeds of glory ;
Till their star in rising splendour
Beams upon the throne of Xiloc.
But she spreads before her heroes

---

* The fabled Atlantis.

Other fields of greater glory,
As she sends their venturous armies
To the Gates of Amalyrac ;
In her hand the gleaming balance
Trembles with their changing fortune,
And upon its beam of silver
Seems to hang the fate of Empires,
Till the parting clouds unfolding
Show at length the final judgment,
Till the fairy vision fleeting,
Leaves the trancéd world in silence.

Listen then and hear her wonders—
Listen to a tale of Fancy :
Listen to the Harp of Pera—
To the Bard of Amalyrac,
To the long heroic story
Of the deeds of great Alonzo,—
To the actions of Gonsalvo—
Of his ever dauntless brother.
Listen to the joys and sorrows
Of the beauteous Amarantha.

I.

GATES OF AMALYRAC.

March of the Islesmen to the Kingdoms of the Eastward.—Their former deeds in Zorayda, &c.—Alonzo leader.—Gates of Amalyrac.—Epiromenes answers the summons.—Parley.—Gonsalvo offers himself as Ambassador.

GATES OF AMALYRAC.

WEARIED with the length of journey,
Wearied with the toilsome marching
Thro' the long grass of the Prairie,
By the dark and lonely waters,
Thro' the high entangling rushes—
Dark Deserta far behind them
Stretching wide its dismal regions,
Lay the noble hosts of Island
In the flowery fields of Thiba.
Few their numbers—but their bosoms
Glowed with old heroic ardour
Worthy of their deeds of valour.
In the sad and toilsome journey,
When the bravest heart had fainted,
They remember'd all their glory,
All the perils they had master'd,
Fair Zorayda twice reconquered,
Northland's bravest warriors vanquish'd,
Proud Dahcotan, long the terror
Of the mighty nations round her,
Routed in her sacred precincts,
Glad to join their conquering banners.
And great Xiloc, she the fairest,
Brightest gem of all the Southland,
With her wide outstretching causeways,
With her tall and gloomy portals,
With her many tower'd temples,

With her pyramids of wonder,
All reflected in the mirror
Of her clear, pellucid water ;
She the terror of Dahcotan
Vanquished by the bold Zoraydans,
Lay beneath their matchless power,
Mourned her bravest sons and heroes,
Mourned the glories of her temples,
Mourned her mighty empire lost.

Young Alonzo rode before them,
Guardian of Zorayda's banner,
Floating free o'er Thiba's valleys,
Flaunting in the freshening breezes.
On they marched, till high before them
Rose sublime a giant portal
Leading thro' the granite mountain.
Bending o'er it calm and stately,
Graven o'er with mystic ciphers,
Stood on either side the semblance
Of an eagle-pinioned Lion.
Full two hundred cubits upward
Rose their forms in towering grandeur,
Witnesses of times forgotten—
Changeless in the flow of ages.
Struck with awe and admiration
Rode Alonzo and Gonsalvo,
As beneath the cavern'd roofing
Clanked their charger's hoofs of iron.
But an ancient brazen gateway
Stretched across the narrow entrance,
Stretched its bars of brass before them,
Staying further passage onward.

Then Alonzo blew his bugle,
Blew a long and sounding summons,

Till the gloomy rock-hewn portal
Shook before the blast of power.
Then an answering peal resounded
Thro' the vault-o'ershadowed chasm,
And a train of noble warriors
Marched in order to the gateway.
Bold and lofty was their bearing,
Rich their arms and golden breastplates,
Brightly flashed their beamy javelins,
Gaily soared their golden eagles,
As to sounds of martial music,
Moved along the serried Phalanx.

On they came, and slow approaching,
Stayed their march beneath the archway ;
But when they beheld Alonzo
On his proudly prancing charger,
When they saw the lordly Brothers
Stately as the sons of Leda,
Then a thrilling cold ran thro' them,
And a dim foreboding terror.
For they knew the mystic verses
Graven on the golden altar,
Graven in the awful temple
Of the Sun at Amalyrac.

" When dark ages rolling onward
" Bring the circling cycles round you,
" When the footsteps of the seasons
" Count the fated number over ;—
" Then before the Northern Gateway
" Shall appear the Sun's bright offspring,
" To require his rightful kingdom,
" To assume his father's empire :
" Partly beast and partly human,
" Armed with thunder, armed with lightning,

"Moving swifter than the eagle,
"Fiercer than the raging lion.
"Tremble then, O! Amalyrac!
"For thy kings must fall before him,
"And the daily sacrifices,
"And the mystical procession
"Winding up the ancient temple,
"Shall for ever, ever cease."

Such the words whose darkened meaning,
Sent a terror through the Phalanx—
For the sons of Amalyrac
Ne'er before had seen a charger,
And they deemed that horse and rider
Were of one immortal body.

As an earthquake overturneth
Towns and cities at its centre,
And its devastating tossings
Bid the neighbouring kingdoms tremble,
So the throne of Amalyrac
Shook before the fall of Xiloc.
Fame with swift and erring pinions—
Sung how she the great had fallen,
Sung how gods had warr'd against her,
Sung the slaughter of her legions;
Changed the roaring of the cannon
Into loudly rolling thunder;
Changed the flashing of the rifle
Into fierce avenging lightning;
And no wonder that the bravest
Trembled when they saw the heroes—
For they viewed in them immortals,
And the children of their Godhead.
Yet it was but for a moment,

And again the hardy warriors,
With a stalworth front and stately,
Waited for their leader's orders.

Then the great Epiromenes,
Hero of a hundred battles,
Victor o'er a hundred cities,
Flower of courtesy and knighthood,
Waving high the Herald's banner,
Tossed his tall plume in the breezes,
And with firm and lordly bearing
Marched alone to meet the strangers.
" Who are ye, who thus impatient
" Fill our fair and peaceful valleys
" With the sound of martial music ?
" Are ye Gods, or are ye mortals ?
" Are ye they who armed with thunder
" Bade proud Xiloc bow before you ?
" Tell us what has led you hither,
" What the guiding cause that brings you
" Thus with threatening ranks attended
" To the solemn Northern Gateway ?"

Then Alonzo, wondering deeply
At the bearing of the leader,
At the order of the Phalanx,
At the white steel of their sabres,
Answered him in gentle accents :
" With no sound of hostile music
" Seek we to disturb your valleys ;
" We are strangers, bold adventurers,
" Guided by the Powers of glory,
" We desire to see your country,
" Wo desire to see your cities,
" And to pass in peaceful order

" To the kingdoms of the Eastward.
" We would hear what favoured nation,
" What most fortunate of monarchs
" Owns with pride such noble heroes."

Then the courteous chief responded :
" O ye offspring of the Sunlight,
" Of the glorious King of Heaven,
" Wherefore do you thus beguile us ?
" Wherefore lead us thus to tell you
" Things that ye have known for ages.
" Ah ! how vain is all the boasting,
" All the valourous deeds of nations,
" All the bravery of the warrior,
" All the wisdom of the statesman ;
" If the fame of Amalyrac
" Has not soared beyond the limits
" Of the azure vault of Heaven.
" Has not reached the Sapphire portals
" Where the God of Daylight reigneth !
" Would ye pass the brazen gateway,
" Ye must ask of Leonarchon,
" Ruler over far-spread regions,
" King of Kings, and Lord of Armies.
" For the lofty portals never
" Ope without the Monarch's bidding,
" Never turn upon their hinges,
" Save before the Herald's office."

Then the leaders of Islanda
Looked distrustfully upon him,
And suspicion rose within them ;
For the treachery of Xiloc
Made them wary in their actions.

But the great Epiromenes
Viewed their gestures, read their feelings,
And with generous warmth aroused,
Thus reprovingly addressed them:
"Sons of the all seeing Godhead,
"Has Epiromenes ever
"Been deserving of your anger!
"By the palaces of Heaven,
"By the Glory of your Father,
"By the Mystery of the Unknown!
"Not a single hair of any
"Who shall pass in guise of Herald,
"Shall be injured or displacéd."

"Be it so," Gonsalvo answered,
"I with state becoming followers
"Pass as Herald thro' the Gateway."

Then Alonzo and his brother
Spake the thoughtful words of parting.
Backward rode the brave Dictator,
Backward rode the chiefs of Island,
And Gonsalvo, with his horsemen,
Stood alone beneath the shadow
Of that dark and awful archway.

II.

AMALYRAC.

Gonsalvo's journey.—The first view of Amalyrac. — Sunset.— The Islesmen pass thro' groves and gardens to Pera.—Gonsolvo, unable to sleep, listens to the song of the Dove.

II.

AMALYRAC.

Slowly moved the creaking hinges,
Slowly rose the huge portcullis,
Slowly passed the neighing chargers,
Thro' the wide expanded portal.
Scarce had passed, when swiftly closing—
Crashing like a storm struck tower,
Sprung the willing hinges backwards,
Shut the ponderous gate behind them.
One last look Gonsalvo darted
Thro' the darkly frowning archway,
Waved his hand in sign of parting :
On he spurred his sable charger,
Wide displayed the Herald's banner,
And all eager for his journey,
Stood beside Epiromenes.

O ! Thou noble steed Arabia !
Often hast thou borne thy master
Thro' the tumult of the battle,
Thro' the perils of the waters,
Thro' the crowds of shouting people,
Thro' the palaced streets of Xiloc ;
But thou ne'er before hast borne him
By such lovely lakes and forests,
By such fields of richest verdure,
By such fair embowered cities,

As upon that wondrous journey
Passed before his raptured vision.
On they rode until the evening,
When their wearied chargers slowly
Climbed the shoulder of a mountain.
Now Arabia gains the summit,
Crowned with many a waving palm tree
Graceful with the boughs of triumph.
On neath many an odorous fir tree,
On neath many a tall Banana,
Rode the scattered troop of Islesmen.
Till the dark wood sudden ceasing,
Veiled no more the forward prospect,
Hid no more the wondrous vision
Spread before the startled strangers.

Bow thy head, O! lofty Strasburg!
Sink in dust ye tombs of Egypt!
Bid thy dome St Peter's tremble!
And thy pyramids, O! Xiloc,
Sink away in awe-struck wonder!
See your giant rivals standing
Calmly in unequalled glory,
Glowing in the tints of sunset,
In the roseate tints of evening.

Far below them rolled a river
Bound with many a fairy archway,
Mighty quays stretched far along it,
Massive piles adorned its borders,
And a thousand pennoned vessels
Poured their riches thro' the city.
On it flowed neath pillared crescents,
On thro' colonnades of marble,
Till it swept beneath the shadow

Of a proud embattled fortress,
Built in old Pelasgic ages.

Rich with shade, and red with sunlight,
Hoary neath its pomp of spires,
Rose the lofty-portaled temple
Of the aye enduring Daystar.
While on high, midst crags of granite,
Fair in all its glowing beauty—
Like an angel guard from Heaven—
Smiled the Parthenon's great rival,
Glorying in its symmetry.
Yet beyond, where great Eurotas
Winding still thro' towery mazes—
Thro' long lengths of palaced marble—
Rolled her topaz glowing billows
To the lake's illumined brightness—
Gloomy o'er mysterious temples,
Dark against the gorgeous sunset
Rose the altar of the Unknown ;
Casting wide a mighty shadow
O'er the waveless sheen of purple,
O'er the gilt domes of the city ;
With its circling stairs around it,
With its long red granite causeways,
Higher than the hills around it,
Like a mountain in the water.

Long the warriors gazed in wonder,
Long they stood in breathless silence,
Lest a single sound or whisper
Should dispel the magic vision.
Long they stood and viewed the Daystar
Slowly sink neath distant mountains ;
Saw their dark gigantic outline

Rise against the far horizon ;
Saw the evening shadows creeping
O'er the glowing vault of Heaven ;
Saw the redness of the sunbeams
Slowly leave the mighty city.
Dome on dome was wrapt in darkness,
Spire on spire was sunk in twilight,
Till the last beam of its glory
Rested on that awful summit,
On the altar of the Unknown.
Then from all the city's towers,
From her thousand domes and spires
Rang a peal of solemn music,
Echoing o'er the distant valleys,
O'er the deep reposing waters,
Till it died in gentle cadence
As the breath of night came over.

Lost in rapture and amazement,
Half afraid to break the illusion,
Moved the noble sons of Island
Passing down the sloping roadway.
As they reached the walls of Pera,
Large and round the moon was rising,
Shedding forth her sacred lustre ;
Half revealing, half concealing
Lovely gardens, fairy sculptures,
Academic groves and alleys,
Beauteous rills and sparkling fountains,
Warbling in the evening stillness.

Scarce Gonsalvo closed his eyelids,
Pondering o'er the wondrous city,
Till the orb in midnight courses
Poured her full beams on his pillow :

Then arose a sound symphonious,
Softly swelling into music,
Like a lovely opening flower—
Like the sweet night-blowing Cereus,
And a voice of angel sweetness
Sung a song in mournful numbers.

SONG.

Lone and forsaken
Sat a poor Nestling,
Calling in vain
For its father to feed it;
Calling in vain
For its mother to warm it;
For they were gone
To return again never,
Gone to the land
Where the turtledoves sleep.

Vainly she wafted
Her half feather'd pinions;
Vainly sought warmth
In the comfortless dwelling;
For the cold night wind
Blew sharp thro' the branches,
Ruffling her plumage—
Chilling all over.

But the fierce Eagle
Heard her complaining,
Heard her bemoaning
Her desolate fortune.
Down from his eyrie
High on the mountain,
Swept the dread tyrant
Careless of pity;

Seized on the soft nest
For his own young ones,
Left the poor Nestling
To die on the ground.

Son of the Daylight !
Son of the Morning !
When thou regainest
Thy beautiful kingdom ;
When thou fulfillest
The mystical promise,
Standing revealed on
The altar of Sunlight,
Pity ! O ! pity !
The Child of misfortune ;
Pity ! O ! pity !
The poor little Nestling.

As the evening primrose closes
Gently with the setting sunbeam,
Sending forth its parting odour
To refresh the fields around it ;
So that sweet and soothing music,
Spread its influence o'er the midnight,
As it sunk in gradual measure,
Leaving all around in silence—
Silence, that invited slumber.

III.

THE EMBASSY.

The Civilization of Amalyrac.—At the summons from the Monarch, Gonsalvo enters the City.—Amalyrac described—The ancient Staircase.— The Guards of Amalyrac.—Passing beneath the statue of the Wargod, they enter the Hall of Audience. —Leonarchon, threatening vengeance for Xiloc, dismisses the Herald of Islanda.

THE EMBASSY.

On the morn, Gonsalvo, rising,
Mused upon the song of midnight,
Mused upon its darkened import,
All impatient of beholding
More of that most wondrous city ;
But the summons from the Monarch
Came not till the hour of noontide.
Wheresoe'er he turned his eyesight,
Wheresoe'er he bent his footsteps,
New unlooked-for scenes awaited,
Fresh amazement seized upon him.
All the beauty of Circassia,
All the splendour of the Roman,
All the taste of ancient Athens,
All the politesse of Europe,
And a science e'en surpassing
The far-boasted lore of Britain,
Seemed all crowded here together
In this fairy land of beauty.
Only in the art of warfare,
In the knowledge of the engine
Moved by vapours of the waters,
Seemed their works to be surpassed.

But a sound of martial music
Rolls along the streets of Pera,
And the summons from the Monarch

Bids them enter his great city.
On they rode thro' peopled suburbs,
On they rode thro' palace gardens,
Till the Red Gate of the City
Frowned in haughty pride before them ;
Far to right hand, far to left hand,
Stretched the walls of giant fabric,
Built of mighty blocks of granite,
Shaming Babylon's high bulwarks ;
Onward still thro' wide piazzas,
On thro' thoroughfares of business,
Crowded with the rumbling waggons,
Crowded with astonished people.
On they rode across the river,
Teeming with a thousand vessels,
With unnumbered fair Gondolas—
Restless with the hum of commerce ;
Girt with many a marbled warehouse,
Many a gilded dome and spire,
Stretching onward till the river
Sweeping in imperial grandeur,
Parted from the gazers' vision.
On they passed neath bronzèd columns,
By the statues of their heroes,
By the fair and stately buildings
Raised by philanthropic ardour,
By their schools and seats of learning,
By the National Museums ;
Under minarets of beauty,
Under monuments of triumph,
To the heart of the great city,
To the Forum in whose centre
Meet the wide streets from the river,
Meet the wide streets from the suburbs.
Onward still they rode, while round them
Rattled chariots drawn by oreas,

Rumbled waggons drawn by oxen,
Stared with open eyes the people,
Trembling half, and half adoring,
For they seemed to them immortals,
Seemed the children of their Godhead.
  On by spacious Market-Houses,
By the broad front of the Mansion,
Where the senate of the city
Plan and build and beautify it.
By the busy marts of commerce,
By the vast bazaars of tradesmen,
Where on either side were crowded
Stuffs and fabrics, gems and brilliants,
Far surpassing England's tissue,
Far surpassing India's jewels :
Till they reached the mighty Staircase
Leading up the rock of granite,
Leading to the Wargod's temple,
That in vast and perfect splendour
Rose enormous o'er the city :
Formed in long forgotten ages,
When he strode the lofty mountains,
When his footsteps shook the valleys,
And he made the ocean tremble.
Now the pigmy race of mortals
Wind in easy passage upward,
Wondering at the mighty Staircase,
Wondering at the hands that made it.

Far along the rising roadway,
Stretched on either hand majestic,
With their bright and polished armour,
With their long spears pointing upwards,
With their tall plumes proudly waving,
With their gold shields gaily flashing,

In the radiance of the sunlight
Stood the guards of Amalyrac.

Now they reach the spacious pavement,
Where the temple of the Wargod,
Where the palace of the Monarchs
Smile upon their mighty city,
Smile upon the lake's blue waters,
Look in wonder to the altar—
Mystic altar of the Unknown.
In the centre, like a tower,
High above the lofty temple,
Like a watchman o'er the city
Rose the statue of the Wargod ;
In one hand he hurled the thunder,
In the other proferred kingdoms ;
While beneath his feet a lion,
Graven o'er with names of nations,
Names of many a conquered people,
Roared with hopeless rage and vengeance.

Underneath the palace portal,
Under painted domes and ceilings,
Thro' long avenues of statues,
Thro' long corridors of pillars,
Passed the herald of Zorayda ;
Till they reached the Hall of Audience,
Reached the great Hall of the Palace,
Where the King of Amalyrac
Sat in state with all his princes.

On a throne of massive splendour,
Reared midst light and fairy columns,—
Shining shafts of ivory whiteness,
Wreathed with gold of dazzling polish—

Sat the mighty Leonarchon,
Lord o'er far outstretching regions—
Monarch o'er a hundred kingdoms—
Emperor of thousand cities.
On his head a high tiara
Frowned with all the weight of empire ;
And his grand and noble features,
And his rich imperial vesture,
Bright with gem-embroidered eagles,
Made him seem by Heaven predestined
To the rule of mighty nations.

By him stood his dauntless warriors,
Wreath'd with glory-crowns of valour,
All their armour graced with jewels,
Flashing back the darting sunbeams.

While around in closer circle,
Worthy of their lordly father—
Worthy of the Wargod's offspring—
Blazed his sons, a race of heroes.

First and nearest to the Monarch,
With one foot upon the dais,
Resting on his gleaming falchion—
Like the terror of the Trojans
Stood the war-approved Araxes.

By him Theron, broad of shoulder,
Panting for a field of honor,
And the young and fair Adonis,
Fleeter than the swiftest greyhound,
First in sports among his fellows.

All along in solemn order,
Lining each side of the building
With their ivory sceptres raised,—
With their long and snow-white garments ;
Bent with age and grey with learning—
With their ephods and their mitres,—

With the symbols of their order,—
Sat the high priests of the Wargod,
Sat the high priests of the Daystar.
O'er them rose in calm composure,
Looking down upon their children,
Thronéd forms of sainted monarchs,
Each one gone to rest in splendour,
In the halo of their glory.
    One alone whose shield was graven
With a dove midst stars of Heaven—
Sign of peace and sign of mercy—
Looked with stern expression downward,
Seeming to reprove injustice.
On the pedestal inscribéd,
Stood these words of deep expression :
" To the Father of his People."
To the good King Philolaos,
Brother of great Leonarchon,
Was the mighty statue raiséd
By Pasitulus, the carver,
The inimitable sculptor.

As the golden gates flew open,
And Gonsalvo proudly entered
With his band of brave Zoraydans—
With his dark and wavy tresses—
Like a tall pine in the forest,
Like a God from high Olympus—
All the assembled princes wondered ;
But when from beneath his eyebrows
Darted forth a glance of fire,
Piercing to the inmost centre—
Searching out the thoughts and feelings—
All the assembly quailed before it.
E'en the lordly Leonarchon

Could not long endure the silence,
And impatient at his bearing,
Thus addressed Islanda's herald :
" Who art thou who thus presumptuous
" Coms't to seek us in our palace ?
" Com'st before us as an equal
" Though an herald from a greater ?
" Tell us what the cause that brings thee,
" What the country that produces
" Such uncourteous behaviour."

Then Gonsalvo, bending forward,
Leant upon the herald's banner,
And in stately accents answered :
" O ! forgive, great Leonarchon,
" That the blaze of such a presence
" Bursting unexpected on me,
" Should have made me for a moment
" Wanting in becoming reverence.
" Lo ! we bear a message to thee,
" Bear a message from our leader.
" We are strangers, bold adventurers,
" Guided by the Powers of glory,
" We desire to see your country,
" We desire to see your city,
" And to pass in peaceful order
" To the kingdoms of the Eastward.
" Woulds't thou know the land whose bowers
" Saw us first arise to daylight !
" Far beyond the blue horizon,
" Far beyond the circling ocean,
" Far beyond the sun at mid-day,
" Lies that fair and blessed region,
" With its blooming vales and gardens,
" With its vast and peopled cities—

"See in us the great aveng'rs
"Of the treachery of Xiloc!

Scarcely had the name of Xiloc
Sounded thro' the Hall of Audience,
Ere the Pontiff of the Daystar,
Starting from his throne of marble,
Cast his sceptre on the pavement,
And with trembling hands extended,
Spake as moved with Pythian fire :
"Open! Open! Heaven of Heavens,
"Pour down phials of destruction
"On this offspring of the Midnight,
"On these dark and impious strangers,
"Who with sacrilegious triumph
"Rifled Xiloc's sacred temples ;
"Filled the holiest of holies
"With the blood of slaughtered people ;
"And, O! fearful desecration,
"Hurled the Sun's most awful image,
"Midst their diabolic laughter,
"Down the steep side of the temple!
"Mighty King! No state of mortals,
"Not the Herald's sacred office
"Shieldeth such unholy scorners
"From the vengeance of the Godhead!
"Take him, bind him, sacrifice him!
"And send forth avenging armies
"To destroy his race for ever!"

Thus the priest with frenzied ardour,
Spread around a wild excitement.
Some step forth to seize Gonsalvo ;
But he stood in stern composure,
Like a mount midst lowering tempests ;

No one dared to touch his garment,
No one ventured ought against him.

But great Leonarchon, rising,
Waved his hand in sign of silence,
And in high commanding accents,
Thus addressed Islanda's Herald :
" Impious offspring of the Midnight !
" This the message for thy leader
" From the mighty Leonarchon.
" Flee away with eagle pinions,
" For with lightning speed I follow,
" Bidding vengeance roll before me,
" For the desecrated temples,
" For the rifled holy places.
" Flee away ! nor seek to enter,—
" Seek to pass the empire's borders ;
" Lest the altar of the Unknown,
" Sated with its slaughtered victims,
"Shall fulfil the wrath of Heaven,
"Shall avenge the fall of Xiloc."

Thus the Monarch, but Gonsalvo,
With a look of awful meaning,
Pointed slowly toward the Southward,
Toward the lofty towered Temple
Of the ever seeing Godhead ;
And in warning accents answered ;
" Think, O ! think, great Leonarchon,
" Of the words that stand revealéd
" On the altar of the Sunlight !"
Slowly turned him and departed.

As the golden portals closéd,
All the trophied banners rangéd

Round the domed roof of the building,
Moved above in ghostly silence;
And the marble kings seemed paler,
And a dim and dark foreboding
Weighed upon that great assembly.

IV.

THE BATTLE.

IV.

THE BATTLE.

Now no more the songs of gladness
Echo from thy hills, O! Thiba!
Now no more the laughing children
Twine their garlands in thy valleys!
Now no more the fierce Desertans
Chase the wild boar through the prairie!
And no more the huntsman's bugle
Rings its shrill notes through thy forests.
All forgotten in thy gardens,
Droop the maidens' favorite flowers!
For the sons of Amalyrac,
At their mighty king's commandment,
At the summons of the beacons,
Redly flaming o'er the mountains,
Leave their sports, and leave their labours,
Hastening to the field of battle.
From the queenly Epidaurus,
Smiling on its lake of sunshine;
From the shores, where Almodira
Guards the mouth of great Orontes;
From the land where haughty Pylos
Holds the dark stream of Eurotas
Bound in massive chains of granite;
From the great imperial City,
With its fair and peopled suburbs;
From the neighbouring states and kingdoms
Poured a host of hardy warriors.

All in line along the valley—
Like the drifted snow in winter,
Lay the white tents of their forces;
And the hum of countless voices,
And the roll of rattling chariots,
And the hoarse notes of the trumpets,
Rose from all that peaceful valley;
Rose from all its fields of verdure,
Breaking Nature's holy stillness.

But at length in mystic courses,
Came the fated day of battle;
And the sun in lurid splendour,
Robed in clouds of red and darkness,
Raised his head above the mountains
Veiled in mist and gloomy vapours—
Slowly rose, as if unwilling
To behold the coming combat,
To behold the fields and orchards
That he smiled on every morning—
That he nurtured with his sunbeams,
Trampled down with armèd footstep—
Lying prostrate in their greenness.
Then the mountain streams lamented,
For they knew the destined conflict,
Knew that ere he set at evening,
All their floods would run with crimson.
Then the tall pines of the forest
Bent before the dark foreboding,
For they knew that ere the midnight
Many a mournful funeral pyre
Would ascend in flames to Heaven.

Now the trumpet's fiery summons
Bids the host array for battle,

Bids their far extended columns
Form into their line of order ;
Bids the deep and serried phalanx
March into its due position.
All at once the winding valley
Bristled with their radiant lances ;
All at once it seemed to glitter
In the faint beams of the sunshine :
Till the hosts of Amalyrac,
Wide outstretching through the campaign,
Rolled their mighty billows onward
Flashing in the brightening morning.
Many an ancient graven standard
Rose amidst their countless lances ;
Many a herald-blazoned banner
Proudly waved above its people ;
Many a brave and well tried leader
Led his native tribes to combat ;
Many a fierce and hardy veteran,
Many a long experienced general—
Many a proud and haughty monarch
Ranged that mighty host for battle.

On the right wing strode Araxes,
In the pride of youthful valour ;
By his side the young Adonis,
In his bright unblemished armour,—
On his maiden field of glory.
   To the left wing, sturdy Theron
Leads to war his dark battalions,
Leads to battle thirty cities—
Chosen cities of the Empire.
   Where the Guard of Amalyrac
Blazed in all its golden glory—
Where its tall and crested warriors
Marched in long and perfect order—

Stood the famed Epiromenes—
First in prudence, first in valour.
In his hand he held the Standard,
Sacred Standard of the nation,
That had led them on for ages—
Led to victory and triumph;
Borne as ancient legends whisper,
Borne by Mars himself in battle,
When he warred against the Titans,
When he warred against the Planets,
When he hurled the Moon in anger,
Hurled it at his mighty Brother:
But the great Unknown, his Father,
Throned upon the Constellations,
Stretched his hand and staid the vengeance,
Turned the vengeance to a blessing,—
Bid it roll in radiant courses
Round the darkened earth at midnight.
Slow it rises on the breezes,
Slow unfolds its gorgeous colours,
Till it blazed before the army,
Blazed a meteor in the Heaven.

Then Epiromenes wavéd
High his hand in sign of speaking,
And sent forth his words of thunder
To the helméd host around him:
"Soldiers! comrades! mighty chieftains,
"Hear the words of Leonarchon!

"'Many a foe have ye encountered,
"'Many a fierce barbarian people,
"'Many a bold and hardy nation!
"'But to-day shall prove your valour.
"'For the foe we come to battle
"'Are the children of the Midnight,

" ' Red with sacrilege and slaughter.
" ' Lo ! the auguries of Heaven,
" ' And the oracles of Wisdom
" ' Give to you to be avengers
" ' Of the fall of sacred Xiloc !
" ' Give to you to hurl destruction
" ' On this band of impious beings !
" ' On ! to victory and triumph !
" ' Fear ye not their arts of darkness !
" ' Fear ye not their monstrous bodies !
" ' For they only add to glory.'

" Lo ! the sacred Standard waving
" Leads you on ! Then raise the war-cry
" Rolling to the song of Battle !
" On ! for queenly Amalyrac."

On they swept. Meanwhile Alonzo
Mounted on his stately charger,
Rode before the ranks of Island.
Few their numbers, but each warrior
Long inured to fields of combat
Seemed to stride himself a legion.
On the right in stern battalions,
Stood the haughty sons of Dacho ;
On the left Cruzatlan's heroes
Waved their tall plumes in the sunshine ;
In the centre far outstretching
In their long and narrow column
Shone the legion of Zorayda,
Shone the long blaze of their rifles,
Shone the bright sheen of their bayonets ;
High above, the dark blue Lions
Danced upon their golden banner ;
While in front the dreaded cannon
Scowling wait the hour of carnage.
Far athwart the sloping moorland

Reining in their fiery chargers,
Marshalled by the brave Gonsalvo,
Rode the horsemen of Islanda.

Then the eyes of great Alonzo
Resting on the ancient portal
Saw beneath its frowning archway
Young Araxes' banner waving ;
Saw the right wing of the army
Heaving its impending billows
Like a mighty brazen ocean.
"See" he cried "my noble comrades,
"See a foeman worthy of you :
"Hard the fight and long the struggle,
"But the triumph still more splendid."

Scarce he ceased, when, like a river
That has burst its banks in flood-time,
Thronging legions filled the portal ;
And from all their mingled nations
Rose a cry of exultation,
As they saw the unequal foemen
Standing motionless before them.
But when speeding, deadly on them
Sang a storm of shot-star swiftness
And in dark and sulphurous vapours
Viewless carnage rained upon them—
Veterans shrunk, and warriors wavered,
Yielding to unwonted terror.
But again the young Araxes
Led them on upon Islanda :
Fierce they rushed—but down upon them
Moved Zorayda's glittering column,
Bore with force impetuous onward,
Bore the foremost ranks before them,

Burst their way through shattered legions
Towards the sombre shadowing gateway.
Then the trumpet's voice resounded,
And Gonsalvo led his horsemen
Charging on their yielding forces.
When they saw them sweeping downward
Like a whirlwind roaring on them ;
When they saw their comrades trampled,
Crushed to death beneath the horse hoofs—
Then they fled beyond the archway.
Flying foes, pursuing victors,
Horse and footmen, heavy cannon
Rolled in headlong torrent onward,
Till the army of the strangers
Stood in grand imposing order
On the southward of the gateway.

When the great Epiromenes
Saw Araxes' flying forces ;
When the refluent tide of ensigns
Poured tumultuous thro' the archway ;
When he heard the thunder roaring,
And beheld the death-shot sweeping
Like a pestilence among them ;
When he saw how few the victors—
Then Epiromenes trembled—
Not with fear, but with amazement—
Then he cheered his chosen leaders,
Marshalling his Guards to battle.
    When the flying legions saw them
Moving on in ardent order,
Hope again returned upon them,
And the remnants of the phalanx
And the ruins of their squadrons
Formed again to meet the Islesmen.

Like the storm wind in a tempest
Howling wild round castle bulwarks;
So the hosts of Amalyrac
Chafed in overwhelming forces
Round the army of Islanda:
But like towers they stood unshaken,
Firm amidst the boisterous raving;
All unmoved, while on their bosoms
Rained a deadly storm of arrows—
Poured a tempest hail of missiles.
All around like sheets of lightning
Flashed the rifle, flashed the carbine;
But the far o'er-matching numbers
Threatened soon to bear them backward:
Then Gonsalvo looked around him,
Looked in vain for hope of succour;
But he saw the sacred Standard
Waving proudly o'er the army;
Saw it graced with golden symbols,
With its gemmed and purple fringes;
And he thought of old Otumba.
Down he bounded from his charger,
Down he bent, and aimed a rocket:
Aimed it with unerring eyesight,
Aimed it with a master's knowledge;
And sent forth its shaft of fire,
Blazing towards the sacred ensign.
On it swept a mid-day comet,
Till it touched the purple border:
In a moment o'er the army
Glowed a dull and lurid redness;
For a moment vivid lightning
Seemed to play above their helmets;
And the Standard that had led them
On to countless deeds of glory,
Sunk in smouldering tatters downwards,

Fell a heap of blackened ashes.

Then the sons of Amalyrac,
Lost in dread, forgot their valour;
Then the forces of Zorayda
Raised a mighty cry of triumph,
And the dark line of their legions
Rolled resistless on the foemen.
Backward bent the yielding banners,
Backward fled the dark battalions,
And the torn and shattered squadrons
Shrunk, o'ercome with awe and terror.
Then the brave Araxes maddened,
Raged terrific through the army;
Urged them onward, urged them forward,
Heedless of impending danger;
Then the sturdy striving Theron,
And the young and fair Adonis
Rushed into the thickest battle—
Darted fearless on the cannon;
Then the great Epiromenes
Raised his voice above the tumult,
And conjured them by their honor—
By the glory of their fathers,
Not to fly like frightened oreas—
Fly before a single legion.

But a cry of woe and anguish
Echoed from the reeling squadrons—
Echoed from the foremost legions;
For a ball had struck Adonis—
Struck him through his noble forehead,
And he sunk a broken flower,—
Broken on a summer morning,
Just when it should bloom the fairest—

Sunk and died—the Sun beholding,
Hid his head in clouds and mourning,
And the sky in sign of sorrow
Wept in raindrops o'er his body—
And the army when they heard it,
When they knew that he had fallen—
He, their loved, adored Adonis—
Staid their flight, forgot their terror,
Formed their ranks and rushed infuriate
To avenge his hapless slaughter.

Then Alonzo saw Destruction
Hovering o'er his wearied army
Bar the way to Eastern Kingdoms,—
Saw his worn and broken legions,—
Saw the foemen onward bearing,
Heedless of the deadly fire,—
Saw the dreaded cannon taken,
All their brave defenders fallen;
And he spurred his charger onward
Where the danger seemed the greatest,
And with stern determination,
Shouted "Death or Victory!"

Through the ranks with arrowy swiftness,
Dashed the dark steed of Gonsalvo,
Spreading consternation round him—
Trampling 'neath him, dead and dying;
For he sought his much loved master;
Sought, to find; for now the hero
Parted from his black Arabia,
Charged to join him through the foemen,
Waving high his flashing sabre—
Making wide a bloody pathway,
Till he met the sturdy Theron,

Hurled to earth the mighty warrior.
    But a cry came rolling towards him
That Alonzo had been taken,
That the noble chief had perished.
    Then Gonsalvo viewed the carnage—
Saw the remnant of the legions,
Fighting still like raging lions,
Falling fast o'ercome with numbers;
Saw the great Dictator captive,
And, unwilling, from his bugle
Blew the order for retreating.

Sadly moved the Islesmen backward,
For they ne'er before had yielded,
Ne'er before had been defeated.
But the sons of Amalyrae,
Wearied by the long encounter,
Ceased to follow at the gateway;
And the sad and broken relics
Of that once victorious army
Marched in silence 'neath the shadow
Of those ancient graven lions,
Mourning all their legions broken—
Comrades dying—heroes slaughtered,—
Mourning those that taken captive
Soon would bleed upon the altar—
Mourning their Dictator fallen,
All their brightest prospects vanished.

V.

THE PROCESSION.

The triumph of Epiromenes.—Amarantha mournfully watches the body of Adonis borne by in state.—The scene changes to Alonzo in his dungeon.—He muses over the Past and the last struggle in the Battle.— A midnight visitation.—He receives the ring from the snow-white figure.

W.

THE PROCESSION.

Gorgeously adorned with banners—
Gleaming in the summer's glory
Shone the great imperial city,
Shone the queenly Amalyrae,—
As beneath her ancient portals
Rolled the long parade of Triumph.
All her marble pillared causeways,
All her tall and stately spires,
All her dark and frowning bulwarks,
All her solemn piles of grandeur,
All her awful forms of wonder,
Glowed with gay victorious ensigns—
Glowed a sea of rainbow colours.
Proudly then the mighty waters
Of the unsurpassed Eurotas
Bid the bright reflection tremble
All along her sparkling bosom ;—
Bid the gaily gilded columns,
And the laurel wreathéd Temples ;
Bid the bannered domes and towers
Of a calm and silent city,
Lay disclosed in azure beauty,
In the crystal of her mirror.
    And the Sun enthroned in Heaven,
Smiled upon his lovely city ;
Poured his beams in dazzling brightness
In a flood of splendour o'er her,

Till her countless gilded summits,
Sated with the beam of glory,
Sent it back again in rapture,
In a blaze of heavenly fire ; .
Till it seemed as though the concourse
Of the starry realms of Heaven
Had descended from their mansions
In the Empyrean city ;
And enthroned beneath the Daystar,
Graced the triumph with their presence.

From the lofty Eastern Gateway,
All along her streets and causeways,
Upward to the spacious forum
Rolled the multitudes of people ;
And above,—adorned with jewels,
Gracing balconies of marble,—
Sat the Beauty of the city,
Pouring down a rain of laurels
On the hero-ranks below them.

'Neath a portico of granite,
Reared above the crowded forum,
With his counsellors around him,
Leonarchon sat enthronéd.
Stooping low, a golden eagle
Held a crown of glory o'er him ;
And his diadem of power
Shone in beams of jewelled brightness.
Round him long imperial vestures
Spread their folds of gold and purple ;
While the ancient emerald sceptre,
Bore on high the Daystar's symbol.
By his side, in mourning shrouded,
Sat the Empress Cleopatra ;
And around on ivory couches,

Shone the beauty of her daughters.
On the left, retired and silent,
Throned beside her royal mother,
Sat the Princess Amarantha,—
Daughter of King Philolaos.
But a veil of silken tissue,
Falling from her gemmed tiara,
Hid her fairy form of beauty—
Hid the tear of sacred sorrow
From the multitudes around her.
For it pained her tender bosom,
When she saw the train of captives,
When she thought how they were destined
Soon to fall in horrid slaughter
On the altar of the Unknown ;
When she saw the young Adonis
Borne before in funeral pageant ;
And she heard the jarring music
Tell how they who fell in battle
Shone supreme in starry brightness,
In the blissful courts of Heaven.

Slowly rolled the bier and heavy,
While the priests in solemn order
Waved their censors spreading perfumes,
Raising dense the clouds of incense ;
Till the corpse of the young hero,
Crowned with laurels, clad in armour,
Seemed to float in peaceful slumber,
Resting calmly on the bosom
Of the clouds that soon would bear him
Up into the courts of Heaven.

Now the loud victorious trumpets
Tell of the approaching army.
See the great Epiromenes,

Reared upon the Car of triumph,
Hailed by the admiring people.
See the young Araxes follows,
Reining in the milk-white Oreas,
With their brightly gilded antlers.
Then a line of kings and princes,
And a stream of long battalions :
Then the heavy rolling cannon,
Taken from the foe in battle.
As they reached the bannered Forum,
And the famed Epiromenes
Passed before the royal presence,
From the crowds of gazing people
Rose a cry of exultation,
And the great bells of the city
Pealed afar their joyous anthem,
Till the ascending shouts of triumph
Pouring upwards, called responses
From the doméd hills around them.

Long they echoed, and their thunder,
Spreading far the notes of gladness,
Reached the cell where great Alonzo
Lay all lonely in his prison.
There he lay, all sad and lonely,
In the dark and dismal dungeon,
Dark, save where the grated window
Let the tardy daylight enter.
All was still, save when the tumult
Of the boisterous voice of triumph
Entered in, in loud defiance.
Sad he lay, but not in sorrow
For himself, his own misfortune ;
For his bold, heroic spirit,
Firmest in the darkest danger,
Stood unshaken by the tempest,

Waiting for a gleam of sunlight.
Yet his mind was bowed with mourning,
When he thought of those whose corpses
Strewed the fatal field of battle ;
As he saw the wasted army
Toiling over endless prairies ;
As he thought how all his conquests,
All his friends and faithful comrades
Now perhaps were lost for ever.
Still he failed not, for within him
Glowed the fire that erst had warmed him
When the viewless hand extended
Tore him from the loved Zorayda,
And he felt, that yet before him
Stood a brighter goal of glory,
And that yet his arm was destined
For the work of hero wonders.

Then the last, the deadly struggle,
Came before his mental vision,
And again he heard the crashing,
Heard the tumult of the battle,
And again with hope undaunted,
Seemed to spur his charger onward.
Round him fall his faithful comrades,
Showers of missiles shade the sunbeams.
Like a cataract, on he dashes,
Through the astonished ranks of foemen.
As a pine tree in the forest
Falls before the forked Levin,
So the prince of wide Orontes
Fell before Alonzo's prowess.
Flight and terror swept before him.
Fear and carnage rode behind him.
Till, alas ! a fatal arrow
Winged its passage through his charger,

And the noble courser maddened,
Rearing upwards, rolled in anguish,
Dying on the field of battle.
From that hour a shade of darkness
Seemed to cloud his recollection,
Till again he woke to daylight
In the streets of Amalyrac.

Even now he scarce could fancy
But that all was mist and dreaming.
Yet the weighty iron fetters,
And the dimly lighted dungeon
Bound with walls of rough-hewn granite,
Told it was no fleeting vision.
  Thus he mused till daylight fading,
Left him in the shades of evening,
Till the moon in cheering radiance
Shed her soft beams through the lattice.
Vain he sought to close his eyelids,
Sleep refused her wonted blessing,
And he watched the grated shadow
Creeping slowly o'er the stonework.
Now it shines upon the doorpost,
Now the iron-plated doorway
Stands confessed all closely bolted,
And the massive rings and rollers
Gleam amid the rays of moonlight.

Does he dream ? or does the faintness
Of the feeble light deceive him ?
No ! it moves, the bolts retiring,
Harshly grating leave the doorcase,
And the rollers creaking dully,
Move along their iron pathway.
Now it opens, gaping wider,
And, behold, a graceful figure

Clad in robes of snowy whiteness,
Shone distinctly in the moonbeams.
Round her neck a chain of crystal
Bore a dove with emerald pinions
Gleaming star-like on her bosom.
Close behind in sable garments,
Moved a form with veiled features,
But her step of firmer bearing,
And her more commanding stature,
Showed her one whom time and honors
Long had trained to queenly presence.

All amazed Alonzo viewed them,
Wondering at the silent vision—
Wondering at the snow-white figure,
Gliding graceful mid the moonlight.
He had heard of ghostly beings,
He had heard of nightly spirits,
That would ride upon the brightness,
That would haunt the lonely prison.
But no ghostly form nor spirit,
No dark messenger of midnight
Could have spread such awe-struck feelings
Through the hero's iron bosom—
Could have sent so cold a chillness
Through his limbs inured to danger,
For he thought he saw the semblance
Of a loved one long departed.
Yet at length with faltering accents,
Thus he broke the awful silence.

" Fairy form of angel brightness,
" What has led thee through the darkness,
" Led thee to my lonely dungeon ?
" Art thou come to warn my spirit
" That the hour of death approacheth ?

"Art thou come to cheer Alonzo
"Through the last impending danger ?"

Then a gentle voice responded
In a tone of heavenly sweetness :
"I am come to guide thy footsteps
"Through the maze that leads to glory.
"I am come to cheer thy pathway
"Through the great impending danger.
"When the hour of death approaches,
"And the priest prepares to slay thee,
"Show this ring, and standing forward,
"Fearlessly demand the challenge.
"Ask no more, for time is fleeting,
"Ask no more, for we must leave thee."

Then the snow-white form bent o'er him,
And he saw a sparkling jewel
Falling from her slender fingers :
Stooping down he placed its circlet,
Gleaming o'er with gems and beauty,
On his hand ; but lo ! the vision
When he raised himself had vanished,
And the iron portal closing,
Wafted cold damps through the prison,
And the moon enveiled in tempests,
Cheered no more the midnight darkness.

VI.

THE SACRIFICE.

Chorus of the Priests as the Captives are led to Sacrifice. — They wind up the ancient Altar. — Alonzo's Comrades are slaughtered. — He demands the Challenge. — The High Priest of the Unknown addresses the Assembly, and tells of Times to come. — The final Judgment is given, and Alonzo is unfettered.

VI.

THE SACRIFICE.

Now at length the night of slaughter,
Sheds its gloom around the city,
And the priests in solemn chorus
Praise the God Unknown they worship.

"Hail! to Thee, Great One, ruling in Heaven!
"Lo! we prepare Thee a solemn oblation!
"Lo! the long lines of garlanded captives
"Wind up the steps of Thy mystical altar!

"Onward we come, and the perils of battle,
"The prize that we fought for, are all for Thy
    glory,
"Look down from Thy palace of exquisite
    beauty—
"The fount of creation—and smile on our city?

"Yea, as we pour out the blood of the victims,
"Bidding its crimson encircle Thy borders,
"So let Thy blessing descend on our nations,
"Rolling the flood of its fullness around us.

"Onward we march in mysterious order,
"Bearing on high the altar of incense,—
"Bearing on high the hallowéd symbols
"Shrined in the courts of the Holy of Holies.

" Death-doomèd captives, pale and desponding,
" Slowly move over the causeway of granite ;
" And the red torches flaring in midnight,
" Casting a hue of blood on the water,
" Show their dark forms in long ranks advanc-
　　　ing—
" Sadly advancing to meet their destruction ;
" But unto us, for whom they are offered,
" Joy and rejoicing shall rise with the morning.

" Bowing before Thee, we bring to Thine altar,
" Loaded with fetters, the Offspring of Dark-
　　　ness,
" Dyed with the blood of the sons of thy people ;
" And blackened with sins, that arising to
　　　Heaven,
" Call for revenge for the temples of Xiloe.

" Humbly we worship, adoring thy presence,
" Humbly to thee is the offering given !
" For unto thee our souls shall be raisèd,
" Praising thy glory unto everlasting !"

　　Thus the priests in measured chorus,
　　Led the dark procession onwards
　　Through the shade of starless midnight,—
　　Led it o'er the archèd causeway,
　　Stretched across the gloomy water.
　　Tall and dark Alonzo's figure
　　Rose against the lurid torchlight.
　　Firm he moved, unchanged his bearing,
　　Careless of the scenes around him.
　　Mighty thoughts were passing through him,
　　Working in the hero's bosom,
　　How to save his brave companions
　　From the agonizing altar.
　　All in vain ! the lines of warriors
　　Ranged along, a brazen barrier,

And the chains that bound the captives,
And the multitudes of people,
Closed up every path of safety.

Now they reach the mighty portal ;
Now they move in slow procession,
Winding up the staircase stained
With the tears and sighs of mortals.
All along the pile was graven
With the mysteries of the Unknown ;
Here an orb of golden splendour
Darts its redly flashing lightnings
At a sphere of midnight darkness,
Falling far to deep abysses.
Here again its beams of blessing
Form unnumbered worlds and planets ;
Here the Sun in smiling glory
Rolls around his mighty father ;
Here the long wars of the ancients ;
Here a world o'erwhelmed with waters ;
Here the deeds of men and nations,
Dim revealed in giant greatness,
Stand engraved along the pathway.

Ah ! how many a mournful captive !
Ah ! how many a dreadful pageant,
Had for ages passed before them ;
As they stood in silent grandeur,
Telling of a race departed.

Now at length they reached the summit,
Lighted with the ghastly radiance
Of the sacrificial fire.
And Alonzo sees with horror,
One by one, his faithful comrades

Bound with cords unto the altar ;
Sees them writhe in pain and anguish,
Sees the priests midst drums and clangour
Rend their brave hearts from their bosoms,
And the flames in flaring redness
Burn their quivering forms to ashes.

All around in stately order
Sat the rulers of the kingdom,
To behold the scene of bloodshed,
To behold the rite perforḿéd.
Many a heart with indignation,
Looked with longing for the season
When the Sun's predestined children
Should dispel those scenes of horror.
But the beam of hope, that lately
Seemed to show the time appointed,
Now had faded, for the hero
Whom their hearts had fondly augured
As the Heaven-decreed avenger,
Stood before them bound with fetters,
Doomed by the relentless priesthood
To the sacrificial altar.
As they dragged Alonzo forward,
Slowly tolled the rolling thunder
Of the bell, whose awful booming
Echoing far across the waters,
Tells the cities all around it
That a mighty foe is falling ;
That the heart of a great hero
Beats the last time in his bosom.

But the long-continued slaughter
Had o'erpast the hours of midnight,
And the lurid flame no longer
Cast its red glow o'er the city :

And no more it shed the shadow
Of the moving forms around it.
For the golden-vestured morning
Fair arising showed the castle
Grandly dark against its splendour;
Showed the glorious Day star's temple,
Rearing vast its stately towers,
Rearing high its airy spires.
Showed the wearied city slumbering
In the dimness of the twilight.

As the priests approached the altar,
And prepared to bind Alonzo
To its sides all red and gory,
Suddenly he started forward,
Turning towards the thronéd rulers,
And erect with God-like presence
Showed the diamond circlet gleaming
Brightly on his hand of power,
While his voice in stately accents
Spake in stern and kingly measure.

" Princes I demand the challenge,
" I demand the lawful challenge."

Then a thrill of icy coldness
Passed through all that great assembly;
And a long and death-like stillness—
Broken only by the tolling,
Solemn tolling of the death bell,
Spread its ghostly influence o'er them—
Till a faintly broken whisper
Circling round the place of slaughter,
Rising into dubious questions,
Told how few had known the secret;
And the quick inquiring glances
Flashing upward from the rulers

To the mighty sovereign Pontiff,
To the High Priest of the Unknown,
Told how they too understood not.
All, o'ercome with expectation
Waited with impatient longing,
Till the venerable Pontiff
Rising with the sacred college,
Beckoned to the high assembly.

He was one whose lengthened lifetime
Had been spent in deeds of mercy;
He was one who bore the blessings
Of that mighty nation with him;
One whose never wearied labour
Warred against those deeds of bloodshed.
Round him fell a sable garment,
Round him shone the mystic girdle,
Round his silver hair enwreathed
Gleamed a band of gold and jewels,
While his aged hand, outstretching,
Trembling held the priestly sceptre.
  Slow he rose, and words of power
Flowed with honied sweetness from him.
From his venerable visage
Seemed to glow prophetic fire;
And his mild eye, gleaming brightly,
Spake of some great wish accomplished.

"Know that mysteries forgotten
"In the lapse of countless ages
"Still remain engraven deeply
"On the records of the ancients;
"Still remain as hoarded treasures
"In the colleges of learning.
"Some are given to be revealèd
"At the will of common mortals;

"Some are given to be discloséd
"By the mouth of priests and prophets;
"Some are given to be conceaᴊéd
"Till the time by Gods appointed—
"Till the time when heavenly wisdom,
"Working in mysterious courses,
"Solves the mystery of ages.
"Know that on the sacred portal
"Of the Holiest of Holies,
"Ranged among the guarded records,
"Stands this granite-graven secret.
"But at length the time appointed
"Bids me to delay no longer;
"Bids me speak the words conceaᴊéd
"To the multitude around me.
"Lo! the stranger must have justice,
"He must have the lawful challenge,
"For 'tis written 'He who beareth
"'On his hand the shining circlet
"'Placed upon the fiery figure
"'Flaming o'er the Daystar's altar,
"'Shall in times of utmost danger
"'Lawfully demand the challenge;
"'Shall obtain the mystic challenge
"'With the elements of nature.'
"Yet it is no easy combat.
"Fit for children and for cowards;
"For the fierceness of the Eagle,
"And the Alligator's terrors;
"For the fury of the Lion,
"And the four-fold strength of Giants
"Must be vanquished by the warrior
"Who would thus escape destruction.
"Only one, as yet, has asked it,
"Only one, as yet, has known it.
"And that one is he, who rising,

" Now enwraps his ancient temple
" In the radiance of his sunbeams.
" He has conquered and we know not
" But that He inspired the stranger.
" How he owns the ring of magic
" Is a secret undefinéd.
" For it hath for ages glistened
" Deep within the Holy places.
" How he learned the guarded mystery
" None can tell, but He whose power
" Showed it to the Godlike Champion."
But a gleam of light celestial,
Played upon the Pontiff's features,
As with rapt prophetic ardour,
Thus his rising voice continued :
"Stranger ! thou has asked the challenge,
"Stranger ! thou shalt have the challenge,
"Stranger ! unto thee is given
"To fulfil the times appointed.
"Unto thee the Gods have given
" Power to rule the first of Empires :
"In thy hand is laid the balance
"Of the weal or woe of nations ;
"For I see a star arising
"That shall dim the solar brightness,
"And I see its beaming radiance
"Cleanse the blood-polluted altar ;
"And I see the crowding people
"Hail the wished-for hour of blessing,
"When the amaranth shall enwreath it
"With its crown of deathless beauty.
"Vain the eagle seeks to hide it
"With his wings of cloud and darkness :
"Down he sinks ; no tear of pity
"Weeps above the outstretched body—
"Lo ! unveiled before my vision
"Stands the glory of the Unknown."—

More the agéd man had spoken,
But his bent and feeble figure
Sunk beneath the mighty effort;
And his tongue refused to utter
All the splendours of that vision.
Slow he sinks; the holy college
Bear him fainting from the assembly
That had hung in breathless silence
On his words of darkened meaning.

But the High Priest of the **Daystar,**
Rising up with haughty bearing,
Bid them bind the impious captive,
Bind him to the sacred altar !
And with unrelenting ardour
Moved himself to aid the slaughter.
  Then the civic chief appointed
To preside o'er that assembly,
Rising, thus restrained his frenzy
And gave forth the final sentence :
" Vain we war against the Powers,
" Whose decrees are ever during ;
" Vainly seek to change the meaning
" Of the signs before appointed.
" Lead the stranger from the altar !
" Free him from the weight of fetters ;
" Bind him with a vow of honor
" That he will not leave the city :
" For the famed Epiromenes
" Hath declared himself resolvéd
" To await the awful combat,
" Should the stranger, basely perjured,
" Break the sacred bonds of promise."

Then Alonzo, standing forward,
Raised his fettered hands to Heaven ;

And amidst that high assembly
Vowed a vow in solemn language ;
That he would not leave the city ;
That upon the day of combat
He would stand before the people ;
And that all should know that honor
Dwelt within the stranger's bosom.
  Then the famed Epiromenes,
Hastening to him, loosed his fetters ;
Grasped his hand, and bade him welcome !
Welcome to his halls in Pera :
Till the Oracle of Wisdom,
Far beyond the snow-capped mountains,
Should reveal the fated hour
Destined for the coming conflict.

Then the long procession slowly
Left the dreadful scene of slaughter.
But Alonzo, turning backwards,
Lingering in mournful silence,
Bade a long farewell in sorrow
To the burnt and mangled corpses
Of his brave and faithful comrades.

VII.

AMARANTHA.

The Gardens and Palace of Epiromenes. —Amarantha sings to Alonzo the Deeds of her Ancestors, of her father Philolaos, and Epiromenes.—Turning to him, she requests him to relate his Actions, to which he assents.

VII.

AMARANTHA.

Fair are all the stately bowers,
That beside the Lake of Como
Lie like gems of varied colors,
Gleaming round a costly jewel.
Fair are all the lovely gardens
Where the brightest Indian flowers
Pour their perfumes o'er the borders
Of Cashmera's waves of silver.

But still fairer were the bowers,
And still brighter was the garden,
Where the famed Epiromenes—
Wearied with the toils of glory,
Would, retired at evening stillness,
Muse upon the works of nature;
Drinking there the calm refreshment
Poured from all her founts of beauty.

Yes! it was a lovely garden,
Fit to nurture deeds of greatness;
When the sun in sinking radiance
Shot its mellow beams of brightness
Through the dark boughs of the cedars,
When it shed the palm tree's shadow
Far along the lawns of verdure;
When it clothed the distant city
In her robes of evening purple,
And the luminous lake unruffled,
Mirrored clear the glowing summits
Of the distant peaks of Deiro.

To the west arose the Island
On whose shores a race of monarchs
Lay in funeral pomp enshrined ;
Pyramids whose steps of granite
Braved the unwearied storms of ages ;
Brazen columns, Doric temples,
Obelisks, gigantic statues,
Traced their forms in dark distinctness
On the orange tints of sunset.
   To the south in mystic grandeur,
Softly melting into dimness—
High above the tall bananas
Rose the ancient founded altar,
While between the reddening causeway
Stretched the long line of its pillars.

Lofty groves of odorous pine-trees
Gently waving moved their branches ;
Flowers of fragrance lowly bending,
Kissed the lips of sparkling streamlets,
That in answer, warbling praises,
Threw a dew of pearls around them,
As they dashed along in laughter,
Leaping to the pool beneath them,
Where the varied lilies floating,
Lay like roses on the water.
   Stately walks and terraced gardens,
Lined with gems of classic sculpture,
Rose by steps of polished marble
To the brazen portalled palace,
That on shafts of purest whiteness,
Reared its pillared domes to Heaven.
   Here a poet's aged figure
Glowed with old Homeric fire ;
Here a Plato bending forward,
Teaches wisdom to the people ;

Here the glorious Philolaos
Gives the sacred scroll of freedom
To the nations kneeling round him.

  But a strain of gentle music
Rises from the graceful columns
Shading round the hero's palace.
  Now it sinks, but blending sweetly.
Hark! a voice is softly singing
Of the deeds of ancient warriors,
Of the deeds of old Almodad.
Is it not the same, that flowing
Through the moonlit groves of Pera,
Poured its harmony at midnight
In Gonsalvo's raptured hearing!
Yes it is, and slowly swelling,
Now again the loftier cadence
Sweeps along in hero measure.
Hark! it sings of Philolaos,
King o'er mighty Amalyrac.
Sings his fame, and how he warréd,
How he conquered great Larissa;
How he won a lovely island,
And returning home in glory,
Gave it to his Amarantha.
  Now she praises all the riches,
All the beauties of her island.
Sings its fields of balm and odours,
Sings its many peopled cities;
How her hills and groves of orange,
Circled by the billowy ocean,
Gaze upon imperial rivers.
Here the broad stream of Eurotas
Bears along a thousand vessels;
Hear Larissa, sweeping downwards,
Spreads the azure of its waters.

Now her bolder theme is telling
Of the triumphs of her kinsman—
Of the famed Epiromenes.
How he led her father's armies
All along the wide Orontes ;
How he bid the waves of Empire
Dash upon Sorardo's mountains ;
How he staid the whelming waters
Of the flood of conquering Xiloc,
And set bounds unto the raging
Of Alloria's iron tempests.

Trembling chords in solemn measure,
Mourn the death of her great father,
Mourn the sorrows of her kingdom,
Neath the rule of Leonarchon.
Tell how all in vain the people,
Struggling with the proud usurper,
Called aloud for Amarantha.
Fruitless strife, the cruel monarch
Bore her, with her royal mother,
Far away amidst the forests,
Shadowing o'er Phoceia's valleys.
Yet at length, his heart relenting,
Placed the crown of Epidaurus,
On the brows that rightly bore it—
On the queen of Philolaos.

Hark ! the voice in sinking cadence,
Fondly praises Epidaurus ;
Sings its marble mansions shining
Round the lake's transparent azure ;
Sings her balmy blooming valleys,
Circled by luxuriant summits ;
Sings the white walls of her cities,
Peopled by a happy nation,
Till the soul-delighting music

Died away in melting distance,
And a peace inspiring stillness
Spread its mantle o'er the garden.

From a hall of classic beauty,
Whose bright portico of columns
Seemed to frame the lovely landscape
In its shafts of twisted silver,
Rose that harmony of sweetness.
  In the centre, amber pillars
Bore on high a dome of marble,
Shimmering o'er with brighter spangles
Than thy gorgeous roofs, Alhamar!
Reared beside the waves of Darro;
Neath its shade a sparkling fountain,
Glowing with the varied sunbeams,
Shed delicious coolness round it—
Waking ecstasy of fragrance
From the flowers that blushed beneath it.
  On the walls, twixt high pilasters,
Shone the works of mighty masters,
'Gainst whose shades of darker painting
Glittered forms of purest whiteness.

Bending forward, pouring sweetness
From the deep tones of her lyre;
In the bloom of youthful beauty
Sat the favorite of the nation,—
Sat the Princess Amarantha.
Gaily flew her fairy fingers,
Dancing lightly through its mazes,
And the diamonds of her bracelets
Sparkled in the light of evening.
  O'er her neck, in flowing richness,
Rolled her light luxuriant tresses,—

Bound with many a costly jewel,
That around her bright tiara,
Shone like stars amid the moonlight.
Round her form of matchless beauty
Fell the folds of snowy network,—
Fell the robes of silken tissue,
Broidered in the looms of Pera.
Round her waist a golden girdle
Clasped it closer to her bosom,
Where the dove, with emerald pinions,
Nestled midst the gleaming brilliants.

But she bids the lyre no longer
Pour around the tones of music ;
And she turns her eyes of azure,
Radiant with celestial brightness,
To the couch where love inspired,
Rests the ruler of Islanda.
He has cast his deeds of glory
At the feet of Amarantha,
And now wrapt in mournful musing,
Gazes fondly on his loved one.
Gently soothing, thus the Princess
Spake unto the lordly hero :
"I have told thee all the honors
"That my Father gained in battle ;
"I have told thee how my kinsman
"Spread the precincts of the Empire ;
"And have sung my varied fortunes—
"Clouds of wrong illumed with blessings.
"Now Alonzo, thou must tell me
"More of thy unwearied strivings
"In the paths decreed by Heaven :—
"Stormy paths, with mists enshrouded,
"Leading by the coasts of sorrow ;
"Leading from the homes of sunshine ;

"Parting thee from Elcorada.
"Ah ! I fear still darker troubles
"Now are rising, soon to whelm thee
"Deeper in their gathering tempests.
"For alas ! the day is hastening,
"Destined for the fatal combat.
"But we must not let our sorrow
"Blight the few remaining hours ;
"Must not let these dark forebodings
"Shade the summer of our blessings.
"Tell me then, my loved Alonzo—
"Tell me of thy deeds of glory ! "

Then the mighty chieftain answered :
"Few, O ! lovely Amarantha,
"Few have been my deeds of glory
"When compared with the greatness
"Of the acts of Philolaos.
"Little worth that thou shouldst hear them,
"Daughter of a race of heroes,
"Yet if it will give thee solace,
"Listen to Alonzo's story."

VIII.

XILOC.

Alonzo relates his Departure from Zorayda and Landing at Cruzatlan.—The Strangers are welcomed by the Inhabitants.—At their Intercession they lead them to encounter the invading Armies of Xiloc.—They are victorious, but are attacked in the Defiles of Dahco; yet her People being repelled, and hearing that they were striving for Freedom, join them in the March on Xiloc, which falls before them. — The Land of Wonders. — The Embassy from Ardoc, and Expedition in her aid.

VIII.

XILOC.

"There are solemn times of parting,
"When the soul is sad and weary;
"When the pathway of our being
"Leads us over desert mountains,
"When the works of the Eternal,
"Radiant in their perfect beauty,
"Cease to cheer the way-worn spirit.
"Such a season, Amarantha,
"Was our farewell to Zorayda.
"For the Power whose greater wisdom
"Guides the destiny of mortals,
"Raised within the Northern Monarch,
"Ever yearning thirst for conquest;
"Dooming the devoted city.
"And although the sons of freedom,
"Gathering from the far-off nations,
"Twice regained the fallen fortress;
"Yet the wise decrees of Heaven
"Could not thus by man be altered;
"And the remnant of her heroes,
"Borne by a mysterious impulse
"O'er the waves of shipless oceans,
"Left for aye the land belovéd,
"Left the shores of Elcorada.

"As the verdure crownéd Islands
"Faded in the growing distance,
"Deep emotion filled our bosoms.

" Hardy veterans bronzed with warfare
" Shed the bitter tear of sadness,
" And the lips of youthful warriors
" Trembled with the strength of sorrow ;
" While the Lion flag unconscious,
" Danced above the helméd mourners.
" Many days of winds and tempests
" Swept us o'er the stormy ocean ;
" Many nights enveiled in darkness
" Hid the beams of bright Canopus ;
" Yet at length the fair Aurora,
" Smiling on unclouded Heavens,
" Showed ·afar along the horizon,
" Hills and valleys, towns and cities,
" Gleaming in the mist of morning.
" Then we saw the beamy brethren
" Shining on our swelling canvas ;
" Saw their starry radiance glitter
" In the faintness of the twilight ;
" And our hopes again arising,
" Hailed the ascending sun of gladness.
" Now we thread the verdant labyrinth
" Of the purple-tinted islands ;
" Now we glide along the bosom
" Of a grove-encircled inlet :
" All behind our lengthened furrow,
" Glowed beneath the clear-rayed morning,
" Till the bay, retiring southward,
" Showed a bulwarked city, seated
" With its ancient piles and temples,
" On the green banks of a river.
" Pressing downwards to the haven,
" Ran in crowds the astonished people,
" Wondering at our towering vessels,
" Trembling at their voice of thunder.
" Till their princely chief approaching,

"Borne on high midst waving feathers,
"Bade us welcome to his city,—
"Regal city of Cruzatlan.

"In the spacious builded forum,—
"Watching all her gloomy gateways,
"Stood a temple, graven over,
"Rudely carved with ancient symbols,
"Scattered in their thick confusion
"O'er its roughly fashioned pillars.
"Here her stranger-greeting princes,
"Bade us rest and taste their bounty:
"Here they told us of the greatness
"Of the imperial throne of Xiloc;
"Told us how her yoke of bondage
"Bowed the necks of vanquished nations;
"Told us how her victor armies
"Marched in pride to break their power;
"And implored us if we ever
"Loved the priceless gift of freedom,
"To protect them with our thunder.
"Then we knew the hand of Heaven,
"Guiding o'er the pathless oceans,
"Brought Zorayda's outcast warriors
"To the aid of fair Cruzatlan:
"And I led their plumèd heroes
"To contend with Xiloc's armies.
"Vainly did the imperial chieftains
"Spread their forces through the valley,—
"Standing in unequal order,
"Gleaming in barbaric richness:
"For a gloomy fear controlled them
"When they saw the armèd strangers
"Masters of the bolts of thunder;
"When they thought the forkèd lightning
"Winged its courses at our pleasure:

"And their yielding legions scattered,
"Flying from the dreaded combat,
"Left their camp, and all its treasure,
"Trophies of our easy triumph.

"But far other was the combat,
"And far greater was the slaughter
"When the sons of high Dahcotan
"Met us in their rocky valleys;
"When the consuls of her people
"Sought to stay Cruzatlan's ardour.
"Long and doubtful was the struggle,
"Long it lasted—till the evening;
"Long the gallant Amphilonin
"Led the hosts of the Republic.
"But at length propitious fortune
"Bore him backwards, slow retiring;
"And their troops in sullen order,
"Sighing left the field of battle.
"Yet no thirsty rage for vengeance
"Glowed within their manly bosoms;
"And when they had heard how freedom
"Was the guerdon that we fought for—
"When they heard how we were warring
"To avenge the wrongs of nations,
"Filled with joy, the generous people
"Nobly pledged enduring friendship,
"And the lions of Zorayda,
"Floating with Dahcotan's dragon—
"With the eagle of Cruzatlan;
"Led the three united armies—
"Led the forces of Islanda
"To the regions of Xilocan.

"Glorious was indeed the prospect
"Of her wide extended champaign,

"As our armies gained the summit
"Of the high impending mountains.
"Verdant groves, and fruitful orchards,
"Peopled towns, and quiet hamlets
"Spread their varied charms beneath us.
"Gently sloping hills arising,
"Bore the waving gifts of Ceres ;
"Countless rills of gleaming brightness,
"Gliding on in streams of silver,
"Wound meandering thro' the valleys
"To the broad flood of a river,
"On whose banks the fleeting sunbeams
"Showed at times the dazzling whiteness
"Of her lofty towered cities.
"Far away upon the horizon,
"Dim amid the veil of sunlight,
"Rose the propylœan temples
"Of the great imperial Xiloc ;
"Rose her pyramids of vastness,
"Swelling o'er the fertile champaign,
"Like the rich embronzed carving
"Wrought upon the emblazoned centre
"Of the sevenfold shield of heroes ;
"While behind, enrobed in distance,
"Traced in faint etherial outline
"Glowed the forms of shadowy mountains.
"Such the land whose fairy regions
"Groaned beneath the yoke of bondage ;
"Such the land whose abject princes
"Bowed before the throne of Xiloc.

"Tremblingly her priestly monarch
"Sought the shade of halls prophetic,
"When the messenger of evil
"Told him of retreating armies,
"Told him how mysterious strangers,

"Armed with thunder bolts of terror,
"Led the legions of Cruzatlan.
"Yet a smile of exultation
"Passed across his royal features,
"When he heard how we had rashly
"Dared the defiles of Dahcotan.
"For he knew the hardy warriors
"Fostered in her mountain bosom,
"Well could guard their cherished valleys
"With the patriot sword of freedom.
"But when he beheld our ensigns
"Lowering o'er her rocky barriers,
"Threatening soon to stand triumphant
"On the ruins of his kingdom :
"Then a boding fear o'ercame him,
"And he sought by deep devices
"To inveigle us in the meshes
"Of his treacherous woven cunning ;
"For he dared not brave our forces
"In the manly field of battle.

"As we marched along the valley,
"As we toiled amid the forest,
"All around was solemn stillness,
"All seemed lonely and deserted ;
"Save when, now at times, the outposts,
"Sounding forth the notes of warning,
"Told of plumes and polished armour
"Glancing mid the darkened foliage.
"Warily we moved in order,
"All distrustful of the welcome, —
"Seeming welcome of the monarch,
"As he sent his noblest princes,
"Bearing tokens of his friendship.
"For Dahcotan's heroes told us

"How the treachery of Xiloc
"Had become a daily proverb.

"All at once the silent forest
"Started with a myriad lances ;
"All at once the whooping war-cry,
"Clash of arms arose around us ;
"But the veterans of Islanda—
"Lightning darting, smoke enwreathéd,
"Stood in lion-hearted valour ;
"And their panic-stricken army,
"Slunk again beneath the shadow
"Of the lofty waving woodlands.

"But the story of our marches
"Through the wide extended champaign,
"Of our sieges and our battles,
"Of the treachery of the foemen,
"Would exhaust the closing evening
"With the long and wearying sameness
"Of their tale of blood and slaughter.
"How Kuzal and great Chobalca
"Fell before our battering cannon ;
"How Tesludo's sacred temples
"Saw their forms in reddening grandeur
"Painted on the crimsoned water.
"How at length our gathering nations
"Dared the last, and direful struggle,
"On the perfume breathing meadows
"Circling round the lake of Xiloc.
"How our days of toil were ended,
"And the gladdening sun arising,
"Hailed Islanda's gorgeous banner,
"Floating o'er the imperial city.
"Saw Xilocan's flying standard
"Fluttering neath the desert shadow

"Of that vast and lonely mountain,
"'Father of the flaming terrors'—
"Spreading floods of scorching fires
"O'er the plains of ancient Mesha,
"O'er the fields of Hazarmaveth.
"Then upon the wavy bosom
"Of the ever-swelling ocean,
"Rose a fleet of stately vessels,
"Guardians of our rising commerce.
"Huge and dark they reared their bulwarks
"High above Cruzatlan's harbour;
"Greater far than e'en the greatest
"Of the ships of Amalyrae.
"Swift they move upon the water,
"Fearless of the stormy breakers;
"Clouds of mist hang o'er their canvas,
"Roaring furnaces within them,
"Bid the mighty iron fabric
"Move the twisted wing behind her;
"Ranged around the darkling cannon,
"Frowning, wait the hour of combat;
"While above, the mystic needle
"Ever pointing to the northward,
"Guides them o'er the pathless billows,
"Careless of the veil of tempests
"Shadowing o'er the vault of Heaven."

Then the lovely Amarantha
Thus addressed Islanda's ruler:
"Unto you indeed is given
"Wisdom from the founts of Heaven;
"Unto you is poured out knowledge
"From the everlasting sources;
"Who can wonder that the nations
"Tremble as they hear your power;
"Who can wonder that their tyrants

"Flee before your mighty standard,
"When the elements in homage
"Seem to hail you as their monarchs."

Then the great Alonzo answered:
"Amarantha! I could tell thee
"Other works of greater wonder,—
"Other more mysterious powers.
"How the cloud-compelling coursers,
"Pouring fire from their nostrils,
"Rolling on the wheels of swiftness,
"Bear upon their path of iron
"Kings and Princes, peers and peoples;'
"Darting now through rocky mountains,
"Soaring high o'er teeming valleys.
"How the magic lines of metal,
"Stretching over realms and kingdoms,
"Plunging under raging oceans,
"Bear upon the wings of lightning
"News of battle, hidden secrets,
"Tales of woe and words of wisdom:
"And a moment only, severs
"Nations, peoples, distant regions
"Parted by the wastes of waters.
"How the giant iron workman,
"Toiling with unwearied labour,
"Ever lifts his arm of power;
"Whirling round unnumbered spindles,
"Crushing adamantine forces;
"Or with lightly weaving fingers
"Gently twining finest fabrics.
"I could tell of dreary deserts
"Spreading far their sandy regions;
"I could tell of peopled cities
"Boasting of unequalled power;
"Tell of ever verdant valleys

"Sung by their adoring poets
"As the fairest gifts of Heaven.
"But no land upon our planet
"Shines with such ecstatic beauty;
"No bright city rears its towers
"With such grand and royal splendour;
"No such people dwell upon it,
"Blessed so highly by the Immortals,
"As recline beneath the shadow
"Of the throne of Amalyrac.

"But I hasten now to tell thee,
"How at length my restless fortune
"Brought me to your fertile regions;
"What the cause ordained to lead us,
"Thus to come with arméd forces
"To the precincts of your empire.

"As our people-chosen Senate
"Pondered o'er the gloom of warfare,
"Threatening from the plains of Mesha;
"We were told how lordly heralds,
"Warriors from the lands of Sunrise,
"Brought a message from their leader.
"Rising up, I bade to lead them
"To the lofty hall of council.
"As they entered, all the assembly
"Wondered at their noble bearing;
"Wondered at their blazing armour,
"Richly chased in gold and silver.
"Then the Herald, bending forward,
"Paid his reverence to the rulers,
"And with stately presence speaking,
"Thus fulfilled his chieftain's orders:

"' Princes, Senators, and people
"' Of the nations of Islanda!
"' We have heard in distant regions—
"' Neath the shade of Ardoc's mountains,
"' How your generous banners waving,
"' Free the people from oppression.
"' Know that now, that blighting evil
"' Hangs o'er our devoted nation ;
"' For the dark ambitious tyrant,
"' Neath whose sway Alloria's valleys
"' Weep away their springs of verdure,
"' Now unfurls his gloomy banner,
"' Shedding thraldom's night around us.
"' Come ! we pray you, come ! and save us,
"' Save the last pine of the forest !
"' Save the last home of the Raven !
"' If ye know the bliss of freedom,
"' O ! refuse it not to others !
"' But, alas ! Ardocan's mountains
"' Lie far distant to the Eastward,
"' And the Empire of the Daystar
"' Spreads between its swelling borders.
"' They, too, prize the gift of freedom,
"' But they will not succour others.
"' Those whose hearts are true and generous
"' Care not for the lengthened distance,
"' Care not for the toilsome prairies
"' That divide us from Xilocan ;
"' All these lesser hardships vanish,
"' In the glory of receiving
"' Floods of Honour—floods of Blessing
"' From an ever grateful people.'

" Such the import of the message
" Brought by the heraldic envoy,
" And we knew that Heaven required us

"Thus to offer life and empire
"In the cause of hapless Ardoc.
"Then the trump of war resounded,
"Rousing all Islanda's warriors ;
"All the veterans, whom the danger
"Hovering o'er the state allowed us.
"Ah ! those noble hearts whose ardour
"Glowed so brightly midst the dangers
"Of that last,—that direful conflict,
"When the blood-stained walls of Xiloc
"Rocked beneath the depth of carnage,—
"They who sought to stay the madness
"Of the long enduring nations,
"As they plundered all her temples ;
"As their long imprisoned vengeance
"Burst on her devoted people.
"Now, alas ! all coldly lying,
"Feed the savage wolves and vultures ;
"Or, perhaps, returning wearied,
"Sink before the mail-clad armies
"Of Xilocan's priestly monarch.

"Oft my mind in anxious sorrow
"Broods upon the brave Gonsalvo ;
"And I wonder if my brother
"Still is numbered with the living ;
"Still remains to cheer Islanda
"With his realm-protecting wisdom.
"But the breadth of endless prairies,
"Spreads its vast extent between us—
"Or a darker—gloomier country
"May have parted us for ever.

"Thus enveiled in clouds and mourning,
"Ends the story of Alonzo :
"Yet thy love, my Amarantha,

"Sheds a beam of hope across it ;
"For the powers, who in misfortune,
"Gave so fair a star to guide me,
"Surely will not quench its brightness,
"Raising clouds of woe around it ;
"Surely have not blessed our meeting,
"Thus so soon to part for ever."

IX.

EPIROMENES.

Evening.—Epiromenes enters, and brings the Tidings of the Day decreed for the Challenge.—Amarantha offers her Father's Arms to Alonzo, who, advised by Epiromenes, accepts them for the Day of Combat.—As they return to the Banquet-hall, a Messenger meets them, bringing evil Tidings from the Northern Kingdoms.—Epiromenes repairs to Leonarchon.

IX.

EPIROMENES.

Thus the two, in friendly converse,
Wore away the silent evening.
Thus they sat and scarcely heeded
How the creeping shades of twilight
Wrapt the fading world in darkness :
How the evening star in splendour,
Like a comely bride adornéd,
Glided down the path of roses,
That the sun had strewn before her.
How the moon's etherial crescent
Shone serenely o'er the water,
Shedding forth a milder influence,
In the silver sheen around her.
One by one angelic fingers
Lit the starry lamps of Heaven ;
And the ever-beaming planets
Trod the measure of their dances ;
Till the unruffled lake in silence,
Ere it sunk away to slumber,
Gemmed its robe of placid crystal
With the semblance of their brightness.
All was clear, save when a cloudlet
Fleeted o'er the expanse of Heaven ;
Like the dim revealéd figure
Of some pure celestial spirit,
Sent, perchance, to cheer the darkness
Of the lone departing hour.
  Now the moon, in fuller beauty,
Lighted up the lovely garden,

Pouring here her gentle radiance,
O'er the lawns and murmuring water;
Casting there a depth of shadow
From the thick embowering woodlands;
From the temple of whose branches
Grateful Philomel arising,
Woke the sweet notes of her praises.
   Thus in soul-united musings,
Sat the two, nor knew the entrance
Of the famed Epiromones;
Till the blushing Amarantha,
Sudden starting, saw the moonbeams
Gleaming on his glittering cuirass.
"O! forgive, my royal cousin,"
Gently thus began the chieftain;
"O! forgive my bold intrusion
"On your hours of sacred converse;
"O! forgive that I must tell thee
"What will fill thy heart with sorrow.
"For the messengers returning
"From the Oracle of Wisdom,
"Bear the fatal answer with them,
"That the fiftieth sun arising
"Shall behold the mystic combat—
"See the stranger-champion striving
"With the Elements of Nature."

Then a deep-drawn sigh of sorrow
Rose from Amarantha's bosom;
But she staid the tear that swelling,
Glistened 'neath her fringéd eyelids,
As she answered to her kinsman:
"Since inevitable fortune
"Brings so near the dreaded hour;
"Since the ruthless Leonarchon
"Still decrees the direful struggle;

"Tell me! O Epiromenes!
"How we best can ward the danger—
"Surest shield the great Alonzo
"From the too unequal combat."

But the ruler of Islanda
Thus addressed the princely leader :
"Noble chieftain, nought avails me
"Save a trusty suit of armour ;
"Give me but a well-tried falchion ;
"Give me but a soldier's weapons !
"And I leave the rest to—Fortune—
"To the power the Heavens shall give me."

Then the thoughtful Amarantha
Thus returned Alonzo answer :
"Wherefore should my father's armour
"Lie all useless and neglected
"In the tomb whose vaulted marble
"Guards his dear remaining relics,
"As at length a chief is given,
"To defend his kingly honor.
"When the people see the radiance
"Of the crown-encircled helmet ;
"When they see the golden corslet
"That was worn by Philolaos ;
"When they hail the ruby falchion
"Round which fortune loved to linger ;
"Then their loyal wrath arousing
"May perchance forbid the combat.
"For they loved my noble father—
"Loved the good king Philolaos."

Then the great Epiromenes
Thus assented to the Princess :

"Know ! Alonzo, he who blazes
"In the arms of Philolaos,
"Stands confest before the people,
"As the champion of his daughter ;
"He who sets the pluméd helmet,
"Circled with the high tiara,
"Gleaming on his stately forehead,
"Stands revealed the stern accuser
"Of the mighty Leonarchon ;
"And arraigns the haughty monarch
"As usurper of the kingdom.
"Though at first it seems to gather
"Dangers uselessly around thee ;
"Though it seems to plunge thee deeper
"In the fountain of destruction ;
"Yet the people, when they see thee
"Clad in the imperial armour,
"Will remember all the blessings
"Of the reign of Philolaos :
"How the glorious monarch led them
"Gently on the path of freedom ;
"How he strove to stay the slaughter
"On the altar of the Unknown ;
"And their fervent love awakened
"In that hour of hopeless combat,
"May avail to shield the champion
"Of the injured Amarantha."

Then the great Alonzo answered :
"What would give me greater glory
"Than to be the chosen warrior
"Of so famed, so fair a princess ?
"What could give me greater solace,
"E'en though dying, than to view her
"Robed in all the imperial splendour
"Of the throne of Amalyrac.

" Tell me, great Epiromenes,
" Which of all the grand memorials,
" Gracing yonder solemn island,
" Is the tomb whose favoured marble,
" Guards the form of Philolaos."

" Seest thou not," replied the General
Of the hosts of Amalyrac :
" Seest thou not yon lofty temple,
" Neath whose shade the reddening crescent
" Sinks into the dark horizon :
" On the morrow, ere the sunrise,
" Speed across the breadth of water
" To the rock, whose craggy summit
" Bears sublime its solemn portal.
" Enter neath the sacred shadow,
" And with reverence take the armour
" From the sad funereal altar.
" I will bid its mournful guardians
" Not to stay thy daring project.
" O ! may victory enwreathe thee
" With as many crowns of glory
" As she twined with favoring fingers
" Round the brows of Philolaos."

Then the noble three retiring,
Sought a hall whose dazzling brightness
Gleamed from stars of light that glistened
In the azure of its ceiling—
Glanced from lamps of varied crystal,
Tinging with their rainbow radiance
Circling bas-relieves and sculptures.
    As they passed beneath the portal,
Moving on in haste to meet them,
Came a messenger, whose bearing

Told the weight of anxious tidings.
First he bowed with deepest reverence
To the queenly Amarantha ;
Now salutes the great Alonzo,
Awed by his commanding presence ;
And then, turning to his leader,
Thus unfolds unlooked for troubles.

"I have brought thee news of battle ;
"News of battle and misfortune.
"All the stately hills of Ardoc
"Glisten with their hostile lances,
"And their firmly linkéd legions,
"Marching to assail our empire,
"Even now have passed its borders.
"Would that this were all the evil
"That a day of woe has brought us ;
"But the voice of rumour whispers
"That the King of Amalyrac
"Has received unwelcome tidings—
"Tidings which he seeks to cover.
"For Araxes has departed
"With a host for far Larissa,
"And the sturdy Theron hastens
"To attend him in his marches.
"For they tell of hostile armies
"Gathered in the Northern Kingdoms—
"Of Vielma's lordly city
"Severed from the bond of Empire ;
"Tell that Leonarchon's standard
"Waves no more on wealthy Aclan,
"That mysterious hosts of warriors
"Sprung from ocean's hoary billows
"Lead the foes of Amalyrac.
"Such the vague reports revealéd,
"Gliding through the maze of distance.

"But the murmuring army wonders
"Why the famed Epiromenes,
"Leader in a hundred battles,
"Guides them not again to triumph."

Then the General, for a season,
Stood enwrapt in thoughtful silence ;
Sternly pondering in his spirit
All the messenger had told him :
Till his words to great Alonzo
Thus expressed his rising feelings :
"See my friend the grateful honors
"That the kings of nations offer—
"See the boasted crown of laurel
"That the princely Leonarchon
"Twines around the victor's temples ;
"No ! I am not even worthy
"To assist him in misfortune—
"Am not worthy to defend him,
"Though I bear the battle for him.
"Yet, Alonzo, I must leave thee
"To repair unto the palace ;
"There perhaps some hidden counsel
"May approve the sovereign's actions.
"For I cannot see the dangers
"Spreading o'er my burdened country ;
"Cannot see her pressed by foemen,
"Ravaged by invading armies,
"And refuse a patriot's power,
"To allay the rising furies."

Then they parted ; he in splendour
Mounts his brazen beaming chariot,
Flashing back the gay refulgence
Of the lamps along the roadway.
They to seek the cooling fragrance

Of the mellow fruits of Pera :
That in jars and crystal vases
Graced the hospitable marble
Of the famed Epiromenes.

X.

GONSALVO.

The retreat of Gonsalvo through the Prairies.—On his return he finds Islanda invaded by the former Emperor of Xiloc.—Uniting with Amphilonin, he restores Peace to the Country.—He leads an Expedition by Sea against the North of Amalyrac—Description of the Voyage.—They arrive at Aclan, which is in a state of Rebellion.—The citizens advised by their Ruler, invite the Strangers to assist them. The Confidence of the People and Prudence of their Princes.

X.

GONSALVO.

Mourning spread its sable pinions
O'er the army of Islanda,
As it toiled in broken numbers
Through the far outstretching prairies ;
As it left the field of battle,
Where their brightest hopes had perished.
Sad, yet stately, midst his comrades—
Calmly noble in misfortune,
Rode the ever brave Gonsalvo—
Musing o'er Alonzo taken,—
O'er the sacrificial slaughter—
O'er the legend of the Daystar.
  And though all seemed dark and gloomy,
Cheering rays of hope illumed him
As his ne'er despairing spirit
Trusted in a fairer future.
Yet at seasons, thoughts of vengeance,
Goading on the care-worn warrior,
Urged him to renew the battle,
Urged him to return and perish.
Till again arising wisdom,
Warning checked his daring rashness :
Till again the voice of prudence
Bid him seek the realms of Xiloc ;
There to heal his shattered forces—
There to gather round his banner
All the chivalry of Dahco,
All the powers of Cruzatlan.

Long and toilsome was the journey,
As the Islesmen slow retreated,
As their weary marches led them
Through the pathless wastes of silence.
Endless plains were spread around them,
Endless fields of waving grasses,—
Dismal lakes and dreary moorlands,
Dark lagoons and swampy fenlands;
Shores from whence the lonely heron,
Starting winged its way affrighted.
And the changing sky above them
Shed its influence o'er their feelings.
Now its veil of misty vapours
Throws a sad despondence o'er them.
Now unwonted awe enshrouds them
As they watch the gathering tempest—
See its heavy clouds of darkness,
Lowering shades of purple blackness.
Now the messengers of Heaven
Dart upon the forked lightning;
And the voices of the thunders
Tell of the approaching whirlwind.
Hark! it comes, and hollow moanings
Fill the whole expanse of nature,
As the storm enrobed in terror,
Sweeps along in gloomy grandeur.
Round his head the flashing meteors
Circle with their lurid redness,
And his dim right hand extended,
Pours afar the floods of water;
While the earth in silent homage,
Shakes beneath his mighty footsteps.
    Yet at times the glancing sunbeams
Shed a cheering radiance o'er them,
And a myriad opening flowers,
Smiling through their sparkling dewdrops,

Scented all the air with perfume—
Streaming ever fragrant incense
From their richly painted altars :
Then at once the spacious prairie,
Casting off its sombre raiment,
Shone in every varied colour :
Till it seemed as though an angel,
Filled with ecstasy of glory,
Had in passing shed the spangles
Starred upon his iris pinions
O'er the joyous earth beneath him.
　And the cloudless sky above them
Seemed to give the mourners courage,
As its dome of deepest azure
Swelled above the far horizon,
And they raised a song of gladness,
When at length their wearied legions
Saw the mountains of Dahcotan
Glowing in the pomp of evening.

But they scarce had reached Islanda,
Ere reports of ill assailed them—
Ere they heard how Xiloc's monarch,
Rousing from his lair in Mesha,
Poured the ravage of his armies
O'er Tesludo's palmy valleys—
Closing round the sacred city,
Once the bulwark of his power.

When Gonsalvo heard the tidings,
Sorrow filled his mighty spirit,
For he knew how spent the prowess
Of his long enduring army.
But he hastened on to Dahco,
Where the gallant Amphilonin,
Spreading wide the warlike summons,

Gathered in her rocky valleys
All the nations of Islanda.
　Hope-inspired, that noble hero
Heard of their returning legions,
Though he deemed their shortened absence
Boded of unknown disaster.
And although when he beheld them,
When in vain he sought Alonzo,
Grief was graven on his features,
Yet the presence of Gonsalvo
Raised again his drooping spirits,
For he knew that he was able
To defend the realms of Freedom.

Then the two in thoughtful council,
Pondered o'er the Empire's dangers;
Planned their prudence guided tactics,
Ranged the order of their marches;
And again the black Arabia
Proudly bore his noble master,
As he led the chosen warriors
To relieve the leagured city.
　Then the ancient towers of Xiloc
Watched the dread decisive combat;
Saw the waves of war and bloodshed
Rage tempestuous till the sunset—
Saw the tyrant of Xilocan
Fall amidst his yielding forces,
And beheld his routed army
Flying, scattered o'er the champaign;
Till from all that mighty city
Rose the sounds of joy triumphant;
Till she oped her festal portals
To receive the great Gonsalvo;
And she wreathed her crown of laurels
Round the brows of Amphilonin.

Thus at length, Gonsalvo, victor,
Drank the full delights of glory.
Yet again his noble spirit
Urged him to the path of danger.
For a strong—a deep affection,
Bound him to the great Alonzo.

Gentle peace, the joy of Heaven,
Spread her blessings o'er the kingdoms,
And the threatening clouds of warfare
Fled before her angel presence,
'Ere the General called his armies
To unfold his dauntless project—
Told them how the loved Alonzo,
In a foreign land had perished,
And desired their generous ardour
To avenge the honored hero.

At the name of great Alonzo,
All the veteran army shouted ;
All the legions pressing forward,
Thronged to join Gonsalvo's forces—
Prayed that he again would lead them
To the gates of Amalyrac.

For the people of Islanda
Loved the memory of Alonzo ;
And their ever grateful feelings
Mourned the loss of their Dictator :
And it proved their noble valour,
For they knew the certain danger—
Knew how weak their daring legions
When compared with Amalyrac.
But they ne'er could be unmindful,
Ne'er forget the debt of freedom
That they owed to great Alonzo,
Ne'er forget their dauntless leader
Who had given his life to save them.

All along Cruzatlan's river
Shone the brave sons of Islanda ;
Shone the warriors of Xilocan,
Eager to avenge his slaughter.
For Azotan's neighbouring princes,
Ever friendly to the Islesmen,
Told them how they saw Eurotas,
Girt with cities join the ocean
'Neath the rays of Eastern Heavens.
First the lordly Amphilonin
Leads to war the proud Dahcotans,
Leads across Azotan's passes,
Serried thousands of his people.

Then Gonsalvo bids the seaman
Of the city man her navy,
Bids the heroes of Zorayda—
All the remnants of his comrades—
Bids the gallant troops of Xiloc
Climb the lofty vessel's bulwarks.

Many a mournful tear of parting
Dewed the passage to the roadstead ;
Many a noble warrior bending,
Bade farewell to his beloved one ;
Many a gentle eye with sorrow
Watched the swift departing vessels,
As the winds in favoring courses
Swell the white folds of their canvas,
As they gaily bore the pennons,
Blazoned with the dark blue lions.

Yet the daughters of the Empire,
Though they felt the pang of parting,
Though they knew how dim the future,
Hung around the bold adventurers,
Still desired not to restrain them,
For the sake of all the blessings
That they owed to the Dictator.

Now the clouds of smoke arising,
Tell of the awakened engines,
And the fleet in rapid progress
Gains the darkly surging ocean;
For Gonsalvo sought the regions
Where the full floods of Eurotas
Dash their ocean mingled billows
On the isle of Amarantha.

All that day the broken summits
Of Azotan's rugged mountains
Rose above the plains of purple;
But the heavy shrouded morrow
Hid the prospect with its shadow;
Till the clear-domed night arising
Showed again the starry Heaven;
Till the silver robéd moonlight
Tinged the hills along the sea coast.
Then the brightly gleaming lustre,
Thrown from lamps and beacon towers,
Or the grand revealéd outline
Of embattled castle summits,
Told them how their fleet was gliding
Past unknown and peopled cities;
Then the darkly frowning headlands,
Circled with the foam of breakers,
Warned them of the rocky dangers,
With their flaming crown of signals.

Then at times the sparkling moonbeams
Glittered over spacious heavens,
Glittered o'er the white sailéd vessels,
O'er the silent marts of commerce!
Till at length the silver crescent
Sunk beneath the blackening ocean;
And the veil of growing darkness
Hid the fading prospect from them.

For the calm diffusing radiance

Of the smiling constellations
Could not pierce the gloomy distance
With its faintly gleaming brightness.

Thus the Islesman fleet swept onward,
Swept along until the twilight
Brightened up the sleeping landscape ;
Swept along until the morning
Rose behind the gentle beauties
Of the hills of Amarantha.
  Till it spread cerulean splendour
O'er the waves of great Eurotas ;
Till it wrapt the towers of Aclan
In its golden rays of glory.
  High above the ocean borders
Rose her diadem of temples,
Gleaming o'er the waves of azure
That attuned their billowy music
All around her quays of granite,—
Round her myriad masts of commerce,
Laden with the wealth of nations.
Lofty domes of swelling grandeur,
Marble fanes of spiry splendour,
Glowed against the roseate purple
Of luxuriant hills behind them.
  Mighty causeways, mighty archways,
Guardians of her crowding vessels,
Bound a sea-encircled mountain
To the city's orient bulwarks.
Far along the bending sea shore,
Far along her bay of beauty
Shone her lengthened streets of columns,
Shone the mansions of her merchants—
All her halls and marts of commerce :
Till again the waves retiring,
Bowed before the lofty headlands,

Where the gilded roofs and turrets
Of the fair imperial palace,
Rose amidst its odorous woodlands.

But the myriads of her people
Thronged the squares and spacious forum,
And the clash of arms resounded
From her tower-encircled precincts :
For the sons of wealthy Aclan
Could no longer bow in slavery ;
Would no longer yield the tribute
Called for by the grasping monarch.
  All in vain her merchant nobles
Oft besought their haughty sovereign—
Prayed him to annul the mandate ;
All in vain her lordly princes
Poured the strain of stern remonstrance,
For the unrelenting tyrant,
Blinded by his vast ambition,
Scorned to hear the voice of reason,
Till at length her stately ruler
Raised the standard of rebellion,
And the brightest, noblest jewel
Of the realms of Amalyrac,
Shone the first of all the glories
Of the crown of Amarantha.
For the people, ever loyal
To the house of Philolaos,
Scarce had torn the eagle banner
From the castellated ramparts ;
Ere the dove's emblazoned pinions
Soared amidst the starry Heaven,
Hailed by their exulting thousands.

Who can tell the mingled feelings
Of the sons of wealthy Aclan,

When the rays of morn arising,
Beamed upon Gonsalvo's squadron ;
Shewed them one by one in silence
Round the castle-crownéd island,
Towering high above the vessels,
Floating on the broad Eurotas.
But their wonder still increaséd,
As the giant forms approaching,
Moved without the aid of canvas ;
As they saw the clouds of vapour
Stretch their lines across the water,
And a thrilling sense of terror
Ran through all her trembling people,
When the loud saluting cannon
Poured their thunders o'er the Haven ;
When the hills of Amarantha
Echoed back the voice of power.

But the ruler of the city
Saw the standard of Islanda
Floating high upon the breezes,
And at once his prudent counsel
Gave new courage to the people :
"Dauntless sons of wealthy Aclan !
"Fear not all these moving monsters ;
"Fear not for the dreadful thunder
"Rolling o'er the subject ocean.
"For I see the Lion banner
"Of Islanda's free-born nations—
"Of those great heroic warriors
"Who endured the depth of danger
"In the cause of hapless Ardoc ;
"Whom the children of the Daystar
"Led across the endless prairies ;
"Who at length were scarcely vanquished
"In that aye remembered combat ;

" When our bravest kings and princes,
" Fiercely struggling drove them backward.
" Doubtless now their gathering forces
" Come to shed the floods of vengeance
" O'er the kingdoms of the Empire—
" Come at length with clouds and thunder,
" To fulfil the words revealéd.
" For the offspring of the Daystar,
" All unharmed amidst his foemen,—
" Safe amidst surrounding dangers,
" Still awaits the destined hour,
" When the crown of Amalyrac,
" Shall again in dazzling lustre,
" Blaze upon its rightful owner.
" Let us haste and humbly bending,
" Seek to turn away their anger :
" Let us tell them how our city
" Hates the tyrant Leonarchon,
" And implore them to protect us
" As we struggle for our freedom."

Scarce the prudent chief had ended,
Ere the shouts of approbation
Rose from all the crowding people,
Ringing from her answering towers.
Nearer still, and still approaching,
Bearing down upon the haven,
Like inevitable fortune
Comes the dark Zoraydan squadron.
High upon the foremost vessel,
Tall among Islanda's leaders
Stood Gonsalvo, sheathed in armour,
Vainly seeking to conjecture
What the reason of the shouting,—
What the cause that led the people,

Thus to hail their warlike presence
With the voice of exultation.
  But a noiseless calm succeeded,
As a gaily awnéd galiot,
Urged along by fifty oarsmen—
Floating 'neath the flag of Friendship,
Left the stately stairs of landing.
Now it threads the crowded shipping,
Now it glides across the harbour ;
Now it darts with arrowy swiftness,
Through the entrance of the haven.
Till the gilded prow reposes
'Neath the war-ship of Gonsalvo.
  Now they give the sign of parley,
And the ruler of the city,
Rising up with all her princes,
Tells of the revolted city—
Tells the deeds of Leonarchon—
How her wrath aroused warriors
Warred against the tyrant monarch ;
How they raised the starry standard
Of the child of Philolaos.
And conjured them by the Daystar—
By the power the Gods had given them,
To defend the injured Princess
With their dread inspiring thunder.
  Joyfully the Islesman leaders,
Listened to the chief of Aclan ;
Joyfully they formed alliance
With the great revolted city ;
Joyfully they raised the banner
Of the "Empress Amarantha."
Not indeed, because the Princess
Was the child of Philolaos ;
For as yet they knew but little
Of the favorite of the nation ;

But because it gave them power
To avenge Alonzo's slaughter.
Then the fleet of fair Cruzatlan,
Moving on again in grandeur
'Neath the unresisting castle,
Bore the blue imperial ensign,
As it passed midst showers of blessings
By the lofty beacon towers,
Reared upon the piers of granite.
O! what shouts of acclamation
Mingled still with awe and wonder,
Pealed along the streets of Aclan,
As the crowding people gazéd
On the lofty bulwark'd vessels :
As they watched the sons of Island
Landing on her quays and causeways—
As they saw their spacious Forum
Gleam with thunder arméd warriors,—
Saw amazed chivalric horsemen,
Proudly check their prancing chargers ;
As they heard the heavy cannon
Rumbling o'er the stony roadway.
Yet they felt a silent reverence,
As Gonsalvo passed before them,
Reining in the black Arabia—
As they saw the noble hero
Moving slow with thoughtful bearing
Mid the leaders of Islanda.

Yes it was a glorious morning
For the sons of towery Aclan,
When the mighty sons of thunder
Laid their power in the balance ;
And the triumph reeling city
Filled with confidence and boasting—
All forgetful of the dangers

Brought upon them by rebellion,
Thought the victory half accomplished
Ere the struggle had been entered ;
Thought to place the crown of ages
On the lovely Amarantha,
Ere their warriors had encountered
All the horrors of the combat.

But the princes of the city
Saw the great impending labour ;
Knew the strife that lay before them,
And retired in earnest council
With the heroes of Islanda.
Then they prudent formed the project
Of assailing strong Vielma ;
For it stood a threatening barrier
In the path of Amphilonin.
Then it was that joyful tidings
Reached the hearing of Gonsalvo ;
When they told him how Alonzo
Still was numbered with the living—
When they told how Amarantha
Was the flower of grace and beauty ;
Told him of the gentle whisper
Of her love for the Dictator.

Then a fair and hopeful future
Seemed again to spread before him ;
And the beaming goal though distant,
Nerved him for the coming conflict.
And he waited with impatience
For the long desired moment,
When his Heaven afflicted brother,
Freed at length from cares and danger,
Should again, enwreathed with laurels
Lead the nations of Islanda
On a higher path of glory.

XI.

ISLE OF DEATH.

XI.

ISLE OF DEATH.

MORNING SONG.

O'er the calm bosom
Of the blue water
Floats our gondola,
Gliding in stillness.
  Slowly retreating,
  The armies of Heaven
  Bow in obeisance
    Before their great Monarch ;
  Bow in obeisance,
    And falling before him,
Throw off their helmets
Of glory and brightness.

Round us arising,
The white spray is dancing,
Floating in snow wreaths,
As we row onward ;
  As we row over
  The motionless mirror,—
  As our arms
  All bending together,
  Urge on the boat
  To the island of mourning ;
    And our voices,
  Joining in chorus,
    Answer the dashing
Of oars on the water.

Hail to thee, Hour
    Of freshness and freedom!
Hour of blessing,
    That spreading around us
Pathless expanses of tenantless ether,
    Binds us no more
        In the chains of oppression—
Bids us no more
    Bow down to the tyrant
Who has usurped the throne of the kingdom.

Happy the people,
    Who rocked on the ocean,
Fear not the rage
    Of a treacherous Monarch—
Happy the oarsman,
    Who, born on the water,
Rides on the waves
    In the pride of his freedom;
Sweeps o'er the lake
    In the joy of his gladness,
Scorning the pomp of imperial splendour.

Thus the rowers gaily singing,
Bore Alonzo o'er the water
In the stillness of the morning—
Bore him towards the solemn island
Dark with tombs of mighty monarchs;
Now they glide with oars upraiséd,
Resting from the toil of rowing—
Now again their arms are straining,
As they reach the flowing current
Of the broad stream of Eurotas,
And again their voice arising,
Sings the lovely Amarantha.

Where is the Princess! the pride of the nation!
Where is the Empress beloved by her people!
Ah ! she is sad in the shades of the garden,
Hid from our eyes by the proud Leonarchon,
Guarded and lone, till time in its courses
      Make us forget
      The fair Amarantha.

Let him conceal her in darkness and sorrow !
Let her be veiled from the sight of her people!
Vainly he hides her, the flame of our homage,
Nurtured in tempests, is bursting to daylight ;

Hail to the nations ! who far to the northward,
    Dwell on the hills of the lovely Larissa !
Hail to the people, who rising to combat,
    Fight for the crown of the fair Amarantha !

High on the crags of the lofty Vielma
    Floats the bright flag of the beautiful Empress;
Smiling Eurotas, sparkling in sunshine,
    Sees it unfurled on the towers of Aclan ;
Sees the great city enthroned o'er her billows,
    Waving with pride the standard of Freedom.

Oh ! may its fringes of purple and silver,
    Joyously welcomed, be borne by the breezes,
That all unwilling, in sullen despondence,
    Scarcely support the weight of the eagle ;

Oh ! may the dove in its Heaven of azure,
    Soar o'er the mighty imperial city ;
Oh ! may its wings of etherial softness
    Wave o'er the towers of high Amalyrac ;

And as yon planet,
All beaming in beauty,
Pours its refulgence
Over the water,
   So may her power,
   Arising in glory,
   Shine in its splendour
   Over the nations—
So may her diadem, blazing with jewels,
Shed its magnificence over the Empire.

Thus their song in fearless numbers,
Told the feelings of the people,—
For the sons of Amalyrac
Loved the house of Philolaos—
Loved his fair and queenly daughter;
For in secret she would whisper
Comfort to afflicted mortals;
She would pour her golden mercy
In the lap of want and sickness—
And though she in humble bounty
Sought to hide her works of kindness;
Yet the people knew their helper,—
Blessed the Princess Amarantha.

Bright the bursting bloom of morning
Oped upon the far horizon;
And the glowing east unfolded
All the beauties of the city:
Showed great towers dimly rising
From the girdling mists of twilight;
Showed her hierarchal temples,
Solemn in their shadowy grandeur;
Showed her crags stupendous outline
Dark above her streets of silence.

Silent now, and chained in slumber ;
But a few departing hours
Would behold her thronging people
Crowding through her squares and causeways,
Hear the restless hum of commerce
Rising from her busy nations.

Now at length the beams of sunlight
Robe the sky in gold and sapphire,
And display the bowery beauties
Of the lake of Amalyrac.
Show its richly peopled borders,
Graced with fair and stately cities,
Show the fanes of Almodira
Rising purple o'er the water.
All her bright and palmy islands
Gleaming like the crowns of Amaranth,
Cast upon the crystal pavement
Of the palaced courts of Heaven.
Wrapt in thoughts of varied import,
Lay the ruler of Islanda,
Gazing on the fairy vision.
Now his eyes in mournful memory
Rest upon the towering altar,
Crimsoned with his comrades' slaughter ;
Now he turns with gentler feelings
To the grove embowered palace
Of the famed Epiromenes ;
Now he views the lake in splendour,
Roll its waters to the Eastward,
And his mind, in fleetest swiftness,
Soars along the wide Eurotas.
Thoughts of far and unknown regions,
Of the armies of Larissa ;
Of the fate of brave Gonsalvo,
Crowd tumultuous in his bosom—

But a sudden shock awakes him,
Calls him to the sterner present,
And he sees the boat is resting
'Neath the isle's funereal shadow—
Sees a rock-hewn staircase leading
To an ancient ruined portal;
And impatient of surveying
All that scene of awful wonder,
Springs upon its solemn death strand.

They whose favoured feet have wandered
O'er the sands of Misraim's deserts;
They whose eyes have seen the glories
Of the pyramids of Gizeh;
They whose souls have felt the pressure
Of the mighty past upon them;
Even they can scarce imagine
All the feelings of Alonzo
As he stood beneath that portal—
Scarce conceive the clear conception
Of the nothingness of mortals
That o'erspread Islanda's ruler.
Round him rose the tombs of ages;
Round him slept the mouldering relics
Of the proudest kings and monarchs.
All their pride and all their splendour
Long entombed in vaults beneath him;
And the end of all their striving
After deathless fame and glory
Lost in nothingness and ruin.
   Here an agéd pile majestic,
Firm amidst the lapse of ages,
Mocks the memory of its founder;
For the slow effacing finger
Of the never-tired destroyer
Spared the tomb, but shrouds its history,

Shrouds the monarch's name in darkness.
  Here a monument, whose towers
Rose to brave the darkest tempests ;
Rose to stand a fit memorial,
To a far extended future
Of some sovereign prince of Empire,
Lies all prostrate and forgotten—
Lies a wreck of moss-grown ruins.
  In the centre of the island,
Coronalled with rays of sunrise,
Stood a pyramid, whose basement
Formed of mighty squares of granite
Groaned beneath the forest foliage,
Heaped by desert ages,—round it :—
No inscription showed its story,
But the legends of the people
Told how, hid within its chambers,
Lay the founder of their city,
Lay the ancient King Almodad—
He the offspring of the Wargod—
He who first beheld the Altar
Frowning o'er the trembling water ;
Saw it rise above the summits
Of the astonished hills around it.

Now Alonzo's hastening footsteps
Threaded through the crumbling mansions
Of the long race of his children ;
Sculptured o'er with forms and cyphers,
Vainly boasting of their greatness ;
For they spoke a hidden language,
Lost in dark oblivion's shadow.
O'er those streets of desolation
Hung a cloud of awful silence ;
Nothing moved save creeping lizards,
Gliding o'er the lonely ruins,

Nothing stirred, save when his footfall,
Echoing through the halls of darkness,
Scared the death-bat from its slumber.

But he now had reached the precincts
Where the later race of monarchs
Rested 'neath their classic marble,
And he felt the weight of sadness,
That had spread its wings above him,
Leave him as their forms of whiteness,
Shone around his lonely pathway.
High above in stately grandeur,
In its pride of solemn beauty,
Bright with freshly fashioned carvings,
Stood the tomb of Philolaos.
Slow he climbed its polished staircase,
Gazing on the lofty columns—
Lost in thought: nor viewed the shadows
Of the mute retiring watchmen.
For Epiromenes warned them
That they should not stay his entrance.
Long he mused upon the sculptures
Ranging round its lengthened friezes ;
Long upon the graceful figures,
'Neath its pediment of marble,
Where the glorious Philolaos
Poured his blessings o'er the nations.

Filled with awe and solemn feelings,
Hark ! he treads the gloomy pavement,
And the echoing vaults around him
Mock the mournful funeral stillness.
On each side the growing dimness
Scarce revealed the tall pilasters
Bearing up the hidden ceiling.
Yet beyond a ray of daylight,

Piercing through the thickening shadows,
Showed the genius of the Monarch
White amid surrounding blackness :
Wide it spread its marble pinions,
Soaring from a brazen altar—
One hand marked the silent entrance
Of the last abode of sorrow,
While the other, raised to Heaven,
Pointed to a crown of glory
Beaming in the stream of sunshine.

Now the gate of death and mourning
Moves upon its creaking hinges,
And Alonzo stooping downwards—
Entering to the inmost chamber,
Stands before the shrouded figure
Of the great departed Monarch—
Stands before the throned presence
Of the corpse of Philolaos.
  None can tell the solemn feelings
Of that ne'er forgotten moment,
None can tell the chilling coldness
Thrilling through the hero's bosom,
As his sudden entrance placed him
Face to face with the departed.

It was long before he ventured
To disturb the awful silence,
Long before he gathered spirit
To approach the ghostly Monarch.
  From the vault a lamp of silver
Shed a dim light through the chamber,
And revealed the royal armour
Laid on the funereal altar.
  Few had owned such splendid weapons
As the glorious Philolaos ;

Few had known so well to wield them
In the deadly field of battle.
Some were made by cunning workmen,
At the order of the Monarch—
Some were handed down for ages
As an heirloom of the kingdom.

Here reclines the full circumference
Of the broad field of his buckler;
Round its orb the circling figures
Shadow forth the constellations.
While a mighty diamond rising
High above its swelling centre
Imaged forth the Daystar's glories.

Here the tall imperial helmet,
With its plumes of waving whiteness,
With the golden crown around it,
Bears the dove with spreading pinions;
Here is laid the ample breastplate,
Studded o'er with sparkling jewels,
Each the symbol of a nation.

Here his long and beamy javelins
Rest against the altar's cornice,
And his tried and trusty falchion,
Glittering with its ruby handle,
Sleeps neglected in the scabbard.

But apart, and raised above them,
Placed upon a crimson cushion,
Shone, unsheathed, a mightier weapon;
From its hilt of sparkling diamond
Darted forth reflected radiance,
And its blade of keenest metal
Glowed like silver in the dimness.
It was one, that e'en the Monarch,—
E'en the glorious Philolaos
Could not wield in single combat.
O'er it hung a veil of mystery,

And the voice of ancient legends
Whispered how that sword had glistened
By the side of old Almodad ;
How the eternal Daystar gave it
To the offspring of his brother—
Bid him keep it, till the season
Of the times before appointed
Should fulfil the words revealed
In the Holiest of Holies :—
Till his children should require it
To regain their rightful kingdom.

  Now Alonzo, bending forward,
Lifts it from its couch of crimson,
And delighted at its beauty—
Gazing on its edgéd sharpness,
Wields it round in easy motion.

But a slowly measured footstep,
Moving from a hidden portal,
Strikes his ear ; his straining vision,
Piercing through the vaulted darkness,
Sees a form approaching towards him ;
And a voice in solemn accent,
Thus arose above the stillness ;
" Blesséd be the Powers of Heaven
" Who have bowed their ears and listened ;
" Blesséd be the solemn hour
" That has seen my prayers accomplished ;
" That has given my agéd eyesight
" To behold the dawn arising,
" Doomed to roll the night of bloodshed
" From the Altar of the Unknown.
" Lo ! the offspring of the Daystar
" Stands confest before my vision ;
" For his mighty hand upraiséd,

"Wields the sabre of his father—
"Wields the sacred sword Phlegathron."

Then Alonzo knew the features
Of the High Priest of the Unknown ;
And thus reverently addressed him :
"Surely dews of heavenly wisdom
"Have thy secret soul anointed,
"For to me the fates have given
"Powers by them concealed for ages.
"And I will not rest from striving
"Till I bid the hated Altar
"Cease to flow with streams of crimson.
"But I pray thee, reverend Father,
"Tell me why thy joy was raised—
"Why thou blessed the powers of Heaven
"When thou sawest me wield Phlegathron."

Then the High Priest, moving nearer,—
Told him all the ancient legend
Told him how the Powers of Heaven
Had decreed to give the kingdom
To the children of Almodad,
Till the course of countless ages
"Shall enthrone a tyrant monarch
Ever hated by the people."
How the haughty Leonarchon,
Careless of the coming vengeance,
Had fulfilled the words of ages ;
How he ever from that moment,
When he first assumed the empire,
Sought to aggrandize his power ;
How he slew the kings and rulers
Who had loved great Philolaos,
And pursued the patient people

With the blood-hounds of oppression.
Till at length the Gods beholding,
Looked in anger from the Heavens,
And inspired Larissa's nations
To assert the rights of freedom.
"Now I warn thee, warrior Stranger,"
Thus the agéd man continued :
"Now I warn thee, great Alonzo,
"Not to trust the wily Monarch ;
"For I know his secret spirit
"Sees in thee the dread Avenger.
"Even though thou stand victorious
"O'er the Elements of Nature,
"Yet he will attempt to slay thee ;
"Yet will seek by deep devices,
"Still to lead thee to the Altar.
"But I pray thee what has led thee
"To the tomb of Philolaos ;
"What has caused thee thus to wander
"To the homes of the departed ?"

Then the great Alonzo answer'd :
"I have come to bear the weapons
"Of that princely hero with me ;
"Come to take them from the presence
"That is throned in death before us ;
"For his daughter bids me wear them
"In the destined hour of combat."

Then the reverend priest responded :
"Blessed be the Gods eternal,
"Who direct the ways of mortals ;
"Blessed be the Powers, whose wisdom
"Raised the thought in Amarantha,
"For these arms will make the people
"View in thee the favoured champion

"Of their much adored Princess,
"Make them rising seek to save thee
"From the treachery of the tyrant.
"Welcome be the day of blessings
"That shall see the crown of Empire
"Rest on Amarantha's forehead ;
"Welcome be the happy hour,
"Though it bring on me misfortune !
"Blessed be the solemn moment
"When no High Priest shall be needed
"To direct the sacrifices
"Hateful to the Power celestial !
"It may cast me forth all helpless,
"All forgotten by the people,
"It may leave my age to perish
"In the darkness of misfortune,
"But the swift departing seasons
"Soon will free me from my trouble ;
"While a throng of crowding nations ,
"Bowing down in adoration,
"Shall behold the sun of Mercy
"Breaking through the clouds of error ;
"But we may not longer tarry,
"For the swift winged day is rising,
"And its beams will wake the city
"Ere thy mission is accomplished,
"For the tyrant must not see thee
"Bear away the royal weapons."

Then the two in silent reverence
Moved the armour from the presence
Of the still and ghostly monarch ;
Moved it from the dismal precincts
Of that isle of death and sorrow ;
And the joyous boatmen gaily
Bore Alonzo to the city.

But the High Priest of the Unknown
Sought again the funeral chamber,
There to pour his supplications
For the friends of the departed.

THE CAMPAIGN.

XII.

The Revolt spreads through Larissa, the North Eastern Province of the Empire.— Gonsalvo besieges the Castle of Vielma, which at length Capitulates, and the Army Marches to the Eurotas.—Anselmo with his Fleets assists the People of Larissa, and aids Gonsalvo at the Battle of the Causeway.— The Victorious Armies march towards Ardoc, but the Forces of Araxes being arrayed in their path, the Battle of Sargano ensues. —Gonsalvo enters Sargano in Triumph.

XII.

THE CAMPAIGN.

Scarcely had the imperial ensign
Of the royal Amarantha
Waved above the towers of Aclan:
Scarcely had the Sun of Freedom
Gilded all her thousand summits,
Ere the eagle-pinioned rumour,
Soaring o'er the wide Eurotas—
O'er the vales of fair Larissa,
O'er the mountains of Circano,
Spread afar the welcome tidings
That the seat of Northern Empire—
That the greatest of the cities
Of the realms of Amalyrac,
Had defied the tyrant's power,
And had dared to be the foremost
In the pathway of his vengeance.
　　Long had all those lovely kingdoms
Groaned beneath the yoke of bondage,
Long had waited for the blessing
Of the joy illumined hour
That should see the cloud of thraldom
Rolled away from their horizon.
And they scarce had heard how Aclan
Raised the Standard of Rebellion,
Ere from all their fields of verdure

Rung an answering cry for Freedom—
Ere the streams of war and discord
Crimsoned all her flowing rivers.

VIELMA.

But again the rising nations
Heard of still more glorious tidings ;
Heard how warriors armed with thunder,
Offspring of the billowy ocean,
Led the joyous hosts of Aclan
On Vielma's mountain fortress.
How the people of that city
Gladly hailed the coming warriors,
And arousing from their slumber,
From the sleep of lingering vengeance,
Filled her sounding squares with tumult,
Hurled to earth the tyrant's statue,
Piled up barricades and ruins,
Barred the entrance from the castle—
And descending to the ramparts,
Opened wide her threatening portals—
And with pomp and acclamation,
Welcomed in the friendly army.
   Then Gonsalvo spread his forces
'Neath the hostile bannered castle,
And arrayed the dreaded cannon,
Darkly frowning at its entrance.
But the favoring hand of nature
Had displayed her wonderous power,
As she reared her mountain bastions
High above the surging breakers :
As she hurled her rocky fragments
To defend the massive portal ;
As she formed the sloping roadway,

Dark impending o'er the city,
Winding up the dizzy steepness
Of the crag-encircled fortress.
And though small, when viewed in **contrast**
With the mightier works of Nature,
Yet the castle on its summit
Seemed to emulate her grandeur,
As it crowned the brows of granite
With the circlet of its towers.

Solemn was the evening prospect
From the cliffs along the ocean,
As that rampart crested mountain
Rose in all its misty vastness
O'er the tumult shaken city;
As it shed a sombre shadow
O'er the waveless bay of silver,
As its battlements in blackness,
Lowered against the gentle beaming
Of the sacred evening planet.

Twice the sun in highest Heaven
Saw the forces of Gonsalvo
Lie beneath her lofty bulwarks.
Twice the star-encircled Luna
Shone on the united armies,
As they rested from their labours—
Rested from the wearying efforts
Of their unavailing valour.

Yet the dimly dawning morrow
Cheered the long enduring heroes,
As it showed the western mountains,
Gleaming with a stately army;
Tinged the Dragon of Dahcotan,
Waving o'er the groves of olive;
Hailed the gallant Amphilonin,
Leading on his glittering legions.

But the castle guarding warriors
Viewed with other thoughts the future,
When they saw the mystic strangers
Crowding to besiege the fortress;
And their lessening ardour showed them
All the dangers of the struggle;
Showed them how the jaws of famine,
Grim with horrors, gaped upon them;
Showed the distant goal of triumph,
Reared upon the wreck of freedom;
And before the wingéd chariot
Of the brightly beaming Daystar
Had ascended to the summit
Of the crystal hills of Heaven,
All the people of Viclma,
Filled with triumph and rejoicing,
Saw the flag of Philolaos
Grace the crag encircling towers—
Proudly paid their vows of fealty
To the Empress Amarantha.

But the great united army
Staid not long within the city,
And before that day had ended,
Helméd thousands, bannered myriads,
Marched along the imperial roadway,
That extending o'er the kingdoms,
Stretched afar o'er hills and forests,
Till it reached the wonderous causeway,
Built across the wide Eurotas—
Leading to the groves of perfume,
Ranged by Larissana's rivers.

For they now had heard the rumour
Of her freedom striving cities,
And they hasted on to aid her,
Ere the tyrant's banded legions

Trod that odorous land of roses
'Neath their mail invested power.

ANSELMO.

But while thus the Star of Fortune
Guided them in paths of triumph,
Other deeds of noble daring
Were performed by young Anselmo;
By the chief, whose able wisdom,
Led Cruzatlan's cloudy vessels
O'er the wave resounding ocean.
He, the friend of great Alonzo,
He, Gonsalvo's loved companion,
Sought to emulate their glory;
And his ardour breathing spirit
Proved him worthy of his comrades,
As his rising genius placed him
In command of Island's navies.

Scarcely had the sons of Aclan
Watched the great united armies
Leave her lofty towered gateways,
E'er the fleet of young Anselmo
Sought the shores of Amarantha.

But he leaves her hills behind him,
Blessed by her delighted people,
As he glides along the current
Of the broad and deep Larrissa;
As he aids her bordering cities,
Crimsoned with the deadly struggle.

Now he sweeps along the seashore,
Driving forth the tyrant's armies,
Freeing all her marts of commerce;
Till the flag of Amarantha
Waved on Araxcia's towers,

Till the mountains of Circano
Saw Larissa's storm-tried seamen
Join the banner of the Empress.

Gladly then, the young Anselmo
Stretched the hand of friendship to them,
For although they ne'er had ventured
O'er the boundless plains of ocean ;
Though they ne'er had steered their vessels
O'er the blue encircling sealine ;
Yet they were a hardy people,
Ever loyal to the daughter
Of the kingly Philolaos.

But the chief of ships returning,
Sails along the broad Eurotas,
Hastening to assist Gonsalvo
As he marches on Larissa.
And he showed his noble prowess
In that dismal hour of slaughter,
When Larissa's haughty ruler
Vainly sought to stay the passage
Of Islanda o'er the river.

Then his ever ready cannon
Freed the hostile guarded causeway,
Then he led Cruzatlan's seamen,
Bearing back the strength of forces ;
Till the legions of the Empire,
Waiting for the favoring moment,
Wheeling round in lines rebellious,
Joined the standard of the nations ;
Till their despot hating warriors,
Panting for a day of vengeance,
Turned on their astonished leaders.

Then the King of Larissana
Felt the sword of retribution ;
Then Circano's tyrant sovereign
Fell before his mail-clad armies ;

And the lines that still unshaken,
Battled for their haughty rulers,
Fled disheartened from the struggle ;
Till the great victorious armies
Blessed by crowds of joyous people,
Marched in glory o'er the archways
Of the far extended causeway ;
Till the war-ships of Anselmo,
Midst the sounds of martial music,
Glided through the spacious passage
Of the mighty iron drawbridge.

But Gonsalvo saw the summits
Of Ardocan's hoary mountains
Frowning o'er the teeming valleys,
And he led his victor forces
To their crag encircled precincts.
For the sons of Aclan told him
How that bold and generous people,
Had with bravery scarcely equalled
In the annals of the nations,
Saved their country from the thraldom
Of Alloria's restless monarch ;
And remembering all the terrors—
All the sorrows of oppression,
Gave their freedom nurtured powers
To restore Larissa's kingdoms—
Land of perfume, land of sunshine,
To their ancient state of splendour.

SARGANO.

But meanwhile the young Araxes
Lay encamped in strong Sargano.

Vainly had that princely hero
Sought by swift descending marches,
To support Larissa's sovereign,
As he warred against the nations.
But he scarce had left the precincts
Of Eurota's favored province,
Ere the hardy sons of Ardoc,
Breaking from their cloudy valleys,
Forced him to regain the shelter
Of Sargano's battled towers.

Fame, the never wearied Goddess,
Daily whispering fresh disasters,
Swiftly spread the gloomy tidings
Of the foe-commanded causeway.
Told how Larissana's sovereign
Fell amidst revolted armies,
How the victors, flushed with triumph,
Sought the pine o'ershadowed Ardoc.

Then the son of Leonarchon,
Thirsting to display his valour,
Spread the order for advancing,
And arrayed his helméd armies,
Moving towards the hostile legions.

When Gonsalvo knew the approaching
Of Almodad's gallant offspring ;
Though he deemed his forces numbered,
Island's thousands twice recounted ;
Yet he felt the deadly combat
Must decide the fate of Empire,
Ere he gained the rocky safeness
Of Ardocan's stately mountains ;
For he heard how Theron's army
Led in long encircling marches—
Camping in the fertile champaign,
Lowered upon the Northern roadway ;
Heard how from the far Phoceia,

Many a myriad of her people,
Sent to aid the brave Araxes.
Passed beneath Lorana's towers.
  And again the anxious evening
Brought more clear the baleful tidings,
As his breathless spies returning,
Told how they beheld the moonbeams,
Glittering on the moving masses
Of oppression's rangéd legions.
  Then Gonsalvo weighed the dangers
That on every hand assailed him ;
But he thought of great Alonzo—
Of the injured Amarantha ;
And his courage beamed the brighter
In that hour of dark foreboding,
As he waited with impatience
For the cheering rays of daylight.

Now at length the rising sunbeams
Robed Ardocan's lofty summits,
In the purpled glow of morning.
Now they pour etherial radiance
Through her mighty mountain portal,
And display the teeming numbers
Of the hosts of Amalyrac.
  Wonderous was it to behold them
Stretching far, beneath the shadow
Of those forms of rocky grandeur ;
Like that glorious golden river
That divides the realms of midnight
From the Empyrean splendours
Of the noon enthronéd Daystar.
Then Gonsalvo spread his forces,
Waiting for the shock of battle.
On the left, the lords of Aclan,
Larissana's valorous chieftains—

Stood amidst their dauntless people.
On the right wing, Amphilonin
Led the haughty ranks of Dahco ;
While the chosen sons of Island,
Skilled in every art of warfare,
Stretched their long and narrow column
All along the lengthened centre.
Gaily o'er their gleaming bayonets
Danced the standard of Zorayda,
And before them dark and sombre,—
Gloomy like unearthly monsters,
Lay the lines of dreaded cannon.

But the sounds of martial music,
Echoing from the hills of Ardoc,
Warn them of the coming foemen.

It was glorious to behold them
As they moved along the champaign,
As their tens of thousand lances,
Shone like stars of light above them,
As their panoplies of splendour
Darted back the flashing sunbeams ;
As the dark cloud of their banners
Floated o'er the warrior masses.

In the front, the young Araxes,
Glittered in his golden armour ;
And the hosts of sturdy Theron,
Surging like a luminous ocean,
Dashed their numbers on the rearward,—
On the gallant Amphilonin.

Then began the deadliest battle
That Eurota e'er had witnessed.
Then the thunder of the cannon
Pealed along the flowery valleys ;
Then the flashing of the rifles
Lit the lurid smoke around them,
And the clouds of flying missiles

Hid the beaming of the Daystar.
Then the shrieks of rage and anguish
Drowned the arousing martial music,
As the hosts of Amalyrac
Rolled upon the sons of Freedom.
　　All that day the Islesman army
Fought with fierce undaunted courage,
And the great revolted nations
Long withstood the countless numbers
That were chafing, surging round them.
　　But in vain the great Gonsalvo
Dared the extremity of danger;
And in vain his charging columns
Checked their forces for a moment;
All in vain the sons of Dahco
Braved the fury of the Phalanx;
And the gallant Amphilonin
Raised their wonder at his valour;
All in vain Zorayda's horsemen,
Dealing death blows with their sabres,
Spread mysterious terror round them,
For the hosts of Amalyrac
Slowly bore Islanda backward.

Then inevitable fortune
Seemed to be impending o'er them,
And the gloom of dark ambition
Gathered o'er the Sun of Freedom,
When a spirit stirring vision
Filled the armies with amazement;
All the hills behind Araxes,
Sudden burst into a glory,
As the clouds of smoke unfurling,
Showed a grandly ordered army,
Blazing in the glowing sunbeams.
Then a thrill of desparation

Trembled through Gonsalvo's bosom,
For he deemed increasing forces
Swelled the numbers of the Empire.
 But a moment raised his feelings
From despair to hopes of triumph,
As he saw the Raven standard
Spreading wide its wings of midnight,
As the cry of "Ardoc!" "Ardoc!"
Rose above the roar of battle.
 Then the hosts of Amalyrac
Wondered at the mighty cheering;
Then they felt the shock behind them, —
Arméd shock of warrior thousands—
Felt the strength of high Ardocan
Sweep adown her lofty mountains;
And their helméd legions wavered
As they heard the gathering foemen
Closing round their wearied army.
 Then Gonsalvo hailed the moment
To regain the lost advantage.
Then he snatched the flag of Freedom
From the standard-bearer by him,
Waving high the folds of silver
Oer his lofty pluméd helmet :
As he spread afar the signal :
"Comrades charge on Amalyrac ?"
Then the darkly heaving army,
Bending down their gleaming lances,
Raising loud their dreaded war-cry,
Surged in long impetuous billows
On the ranks of Leonarchon.
 Then the legions of Zorayda
Hurled again the bolts of thunder ;
Then the army of Araxes
Felt the victor sword of Ardoc,
And o'ercome with growing terror,

Wavered backward, wavered forward ;
Till the warriors of Phoceia
Shrunk beneath the coming slaughter,
And the children of Almodad
Saw the serried Phalanx broken—
All their mighty armies failing.

Yet in vain their princely ardour
Labored to restore the battle ;
For the horsemen of Islanda,
Led by Amphilonin's valour,
Dashed again in fury on them :
Then their panoplies of brightness
Darted back the evening radiance,
Then their godlike ranks descending,
Filled the foe with consternation.
As they bended from their saddles—
Hurrying on the scattered legions,
Trampling down the flying masses ;
Till Ardocan's forest mountains
Answered the triumphant war-cries
Of the two united armies ;—
Echoed back the thundering cheering
For the child of Philolaos,
As Islanda and Ardocan
Entered the forsaken bulwarks
Of the well entrenched Sargano.

Then the noble chiefs of Ardoc
Felt the grateful hand of Island,
As Gonsalvo and his leaders
Thanked them for their generous succour,—
Told how war arrayed Misfortune,
Standing at the Lion Gateway,
Barred the pathway to performing
What their willing hearts had promised.

But it was not long they tarried
'Neath the shelter of the fortress,
For they knew how fortune's favors
Hang upon the passing moment.
Now already Amphilonin,
Following, tracks the young Araxes,
While Gonsalvo on the morrow,
Marches with his chosen warriors
To the ever bright Eurotas :
Where the vessels of Anselmo
Filled her trembling shores with wonder.

 For the friendly sons of Ardoc,
Resting 'neath Sargano's towers,
Told him of the mighty Pylos,—
Told him how the giant fortress
Watched the crag o'ershadowed entrance
To the sapphire floods encircling
All the quays of Amalyrac ;—
Told him how their southern army,
Marshalled by the sage Leascar—
By their agéd, honoréd ruler,
Hovered o'er the blooming valleys,
Stretched beneath its rampired bulwarks.

Thus as oft the golden sunbeams,
Shine in brighter, fairer glory,
When they pierce the sable tempests,
Rolled in solemn night before them.
 So the glory of Islanda
Burst into a greater splendour
As it rose again victorious
From the shades of woe that dimmed it
At the gates of Amalyrac.

LEONARCHON.

XIII.

LEONARCHON.

Terraced on a spacious pavement,
Vast above the mighty city,
Rose the glorious Daystar's temple.
Stately towers of awful grandeur,
Lofty spires of airy lightness,
Pointed upwards to the mansions
Where He sits enthroned in Heaven.
Endless rows of pillared arches,
Endless tiers of flowing tracery,
Endless forms of classic sculpture,
Countless pinnacles and turrets
Graced the beauty of its outline ;
While the giant eastern portal,
Guarded by its four-fold towers—
Emblems of the four-fold seasons,
Tranced the astonished eye in wonder,
As it gazed upon the shadowing
Of the widely spreading archways.
   But the vision screened behind it,
When the marvelling votary entered,
Filled his soul with deeper reverence ;
As it showed titanic columns,
Ranged in majesty of order,
Showed them four by four progressive,
Bear on high the vaulted roofing ;
As the dim light of the windows

Shed a solemn glow around it,
Casting richly colored shadows
O'er the carvings and mosaics.
   But that dimness too was shaded,
As the pavement wrapt in darkness,
Rose in flights of granite upwards
To the elevated precincts
Where the sombre veil descending
Hid the Holiest of Holies.
   But the folds of broidered tissue
Scarcely screened the blazing splendours
Shrined within its gorgeous shadow;
Scarce could hide the dazzling radiance
Of the semblance of the Daystar,
That on days of solemn worship
Shone before the adoring people.
'Neath a canopy of crystal,
Borne on shafts of heavenly sapphire,
Flamed the figure of the Godhead
Formed of ever burning brightness;
Showing forth the golden altar,
Graven with the words of wonder—
Dark against its pure resplendence.

Close behind the holy places
Rose a lofty archéd chamber,
Where the haughty Leonarchon
Oft retired to sit in council,
With the few to whom the secrets
Of his inmost soul were opened.
It was 'neath its gloomy vaulting
That the conclave now assembled
To advise the wavering monarch.
   Few of all his kings and princes
Know the mind of Leonarchon;
Few indeed had he entrusted

With the secrets of his bosom.
But upon this dark occasion
Three, alone were seated with him.
  Here the High Priest of the **Daystar**
Lent upon his sacred sceptre :
Here the Hierarch of the Wargod,
Bending forward, whispered to him ;
While obsequiously smiling,
On the left hand of his sovereign
Sat the wily fawning favorite,
Ruler of the wide Orontes :—
She who mourned her princely hero
Slain in battle by Alonzo.

But the vengeance brooding monarch
Chains them all in deep attention,
As he thus with shameless freedom
Tells his tyrant thoughts and sorrows.
"Thirty suns have rolled their courses
"Since the troublous tidings reached us
"Of Larissa's rebel armies.
"Then the vague and floating rumours
"Scarcely traced the wide misfortune ;
"Only whispered of the falling
"Of the city of Vielma—
"Of the loss of towery Aclan.
"Now more certain news afflicts me,
"Sent by Araxeia's monarch ;
"Tidings that the northern nations,
"Talking of their rights of freedom,
"Have refused to pay the tribute
"Layed by Empire law upon them :
"And forgetful of allegiance,
"Raise the standard of rebellion,
"Boasting soon to place the diadem
"On the brows of Amarantha.

" Who has ever seen a woman
" Born to rule a mighty nation !
" O ! that, that ambitious Princess,
" With her wiles and winning presence,
" Long had gone to greet her father !
" For her very form reminds me
" Of the day when Philolaos
" Fell before the creeping poison.
" There will be no strength of Empire
" Till she too is laid to slumber,
" Till she too has sought the mansions
" Of the ancient kings and heroes.
" But my wandering mind has led me
" From the deeds of the rebellion.
" Scarcely had the rising people
" Filled the province with their uproar,
" Ere an army borne by ocean,
" Lands upon the shores of Aclan ;
" Scarce had they approached the city,
" Ere the rebels, lost to reason,
" Pray the assailants of their country
" To unite with them in battle.
" They at once delighted listen,
" Smiling at the nation's folly,
" And the invaders banner flaunteth
" On the second seat of Empire.
" Now the two united armies
" March upon the strong Vielma :
" There again the fickle rabble
" Rising up, expel their rulers,
" And deluded by the strangers,
" Think they fight for Amarantha.
" Other rumours daily tell us
" Of some fresh revolted city,
" While the treacherous sons of Ardoc,—
" Whom alas ! Alloria's monarch

"Could not long retain in thraldom,
"Pour from all their lofty mountains,
"Preying on the wounded kingdoms
"With such fury, that Araxes
"Has advancing, left the shelter
"Of Sargano's rampired city.
"Such the perils of the Empire,
"Sprung from our untimely mercy
"To that haughty restless Princess.
"Not sufficed with wars and bloodshed,
"Now she scorns the Powers of Heaven,
"Seeking to defend that captive
"Seared with sacrilege and slaughter.
"I shall never rest in quiet,
"Ne'er enjoy a peaceful slumber,
"Till I know that death has silenced
"All those prophecies and bodings
"That would make the impious Stranger
"Offspring of the glorious Daystar!
"Well, we know he is but mortal,
"Yet the people, in their folly,
"Credit all the basest falsehoods.
"Now I ask you to advise me,
"With the wisdom of your counsels,
"How I best may free my kingdom
"From the dangers striding o'er it."

For a season, thoughtful silence
Reigned within the vaulted chamber,
Till the High Priest of the Daystar,
Slowly thus addressed the Monarch:
"Leonarchon, all these troubles,
"All this discord and rebellion,
"Rise from one great fount of evil—
"Rise around thee for neglecting
"To avenge the profanation

"Of Xilocan's sacred altars.
"No! the Gods will never bless thee,
"Ne'er confirm thee in thy kingdom,
"Till their anger is appeaséd
"With the heart blood of that stranger
"Who has sought to spread dishonor
"On the worship of the Unknown—
"On the holy sacrifices
"That have been decreed for ages.
"For when all the powers of Heaven
"Gave the kingdom to Almodad,
"To the offspring of the Wargod,
"They to stay the raging anger
"Of the Spirit of the Midnight—
"Envious of his mighty brothers,
"Laid a vow upon the Monarch,
"In the name of all his children,
"That the blood of every captive,
"Vanquished on the field of battle.
"Shall be offered up in darkness
"On the altar of the Unknown ;
"Made him call down imprecations
"On the Heaven despising sovereign,
"Who shall dare to break the compact
"Ere the Time before appointed.
"Even should this child of darkness
"Conquer all the varied dangers,
"All the terrors of the challenge ;
"Yet no peace will rest upon thee
"Till his blood hath dyed the granite
"Of the sacrificial altar."

Thus the priest, with artful language,
Fanned the Monarch's superstition,
But the ruler of Orontes,
As he watched his sovereign's features,

Knew the signet of approval,
And submissive, thus addressed him :
"Mighty Monarch, who can question
"That the venerable Pontiff
"Speaks the words of truth and wisdom.
"First of all the thrones of Heaven
"Must behold their wrath appeaséd ;
"Though Alonzo dares the challenge,
"All in vain he wards their vengeance.
"Even should the powers of Darkness
"Aid him in the hour of danger,
"Yet command thy guards to bind him
"As an offering for the Unknown.
"For the fickle-minded people,
"Even though they praise his valour,
"Will by eloquence persuaded—
"Think the combat only gave him
"Respite from impending justice—
"Only gives him longer season
"To repent and seek forgiveness.
"But, illustrious Leonarchon,
"Listen to my earnest counsel.
"Is it not forbid by wisdom,
"That the Guards of Amalyrac,
"Bound to that Epiromenes,
"Should behold us seize Alonzo.
"Rather let them spend their powers
"In the aid of great Araxes,
"While I fill the imperial city
"With the legions of Orontes
"Ever faithful to their Sovereign.
"Give me then thy royal mandate,
"And the sunrise shall behold him
"Lifeless on the mystic Altar—
"Shall behold this child of sunlight
"Gone to seek his Father's mansions."

Then the willing Leonarchon,
Thus approvingly assented :
" Faithful friend, thy timely counsel
" Has relieved my burdened spirit,
" And shouldst thou perform thy promise,
" Nations envying shall behold thee,
" For I give thee all the honors
" Of the famed Epiromenes.
" Well I know his knightly prowess,
" Know his patriotic ardour :
" E'en the cause of Amarantha
" Scarce could make him rise against me,
" For he shrinks from all the horrors,
" Crowded in the train of Discord.
" Yet he stands the great Protector
" Of the house of Philolaos,
" And while he remains in power,
" While he leads the hosts of Empire,
" It will never be forgotten
" That another house is seated
" On the throne of Amalyrac.
" When the General knew the tidings
" Of the great revolted cities,
" When he heard how my Araxes
" Had departed with the army,
" Then he came at once and offered
" Aid to calm the Empire's troubles ;
" But I chid him as a traitor,
" As associate of the rebels ;
" Bade him to depart my presence,
" Lest my vengeance overtake him.
" But he stood as if unheeding,
" Speaking with intrusive boldness—
" Told me how the burdened people
" Long had borne the weight of bondage—
" Urged me to restrain resentment,—

"Urged to offer grace and pardon—
"Warning that despotic power
"Could not curb the Northern Kingdoms;
"And conjured me by my Fathers,
"If I sought to reign in glory,
"Blessed by all the subject nations,
"To remove the yoke of iron
"Laid upon the sinking Empire,
"But again my rising anger
"Bid him cease his ill-timed counsels,
"Bid him haste and join the rebels
"If he loved their cause so dearly.
"Then he slowly left my presence,
"But before he reached the portal,
"Thus insultingly addressed me :
" 'Leonarchon! when the people,
" 'Bursting all the chains of reverence,
" 'Rush on their anointed sovereign,
" 'Then remember how I warned thee,
" 'How of all thy kings and leaders,
" 'One alone was faithful to thee,
" 'One alone has braved thine anger,
" 'As he spreads the truth before thee.'
"Thus he dared with fearless language,
"To upraid me in my palace,
"And though I allow his valour,
"I detest him for his freedom,
"And my vengeance shall not tarry
"Till I see Epiromenes
"Stripped of all his boasted laurels.
"Yet the Princess Amarantha,
"First of all must be removéd,
"First of all the people's darling
"Must be hid for ever from them :
"Vainly have Phoceia's forests
"Veiled her in their robes of verdure,

"Vainly have the palace gardens
"Spread their lonely stillness round her;
"We must choose a surer pilot
"If we would attain the haven,
"We must find a straighter pathway
"If we would relieve the city."

Then with dark and stern expression,
Spoke the Hierarch of the Wargod:
"Let it not be told I pray thee,
"That the Lordly Leonarchon
"Faltered, when a faithless Princess
"Checked him in the path of glory.
"Philolaos fell before thee,
"Wherefore should'st thou spare his daughter.
"Vaulted dungeons lie concealéd
"'Neath the temple of the Wargod,
"Known to me alone of mortals;
"Hide her in their dark seclusion,
"And if still she rouses tumults,
"Still disturbs the peace of Empire,
"There are dismal cells besides them,
"Buried in their walls of granite;
"They will give thee final respite
"From the dark designs she fosters."

Thus his gloomy spirit counselled,
And the Monarch, blind to mercy,
Gave the nod of approbation,
As the Hierarch thus continued:
"Leonarchon, should the people,
"Calling for her rise against thee,
"Should the nations from Sorardo
"To the mountains of Circano,
"Seek to wrench the sceptre from thee;
"Even then thou need'st not tremble,
"Need'st not fear their fiercest raging,

"For the Monarch of Alloria
"Long has formed the compact with thee.
"Ironama's Prince shall aid thee
"With his serried strength of warriors,
"And the dark King of Mediro
"Haste to join thee with his armies."

But the ruler of Orontes,
Bowing low addressed the Monarch :
"Think not, O ! my King ! I pray thee,
"That because the Northern Kingdoms,
"Thus revolting, rise against thee,
"Oro's wide extended nations
"Look with sympathy upon them.
"No ! they ever will be loyal
"To the offspring of Almodad ;
"Ever faithful to their Monarch,
"They will crowd to fight his battles ;
"Even now her veteran legions
"Gather by the great Orontes,
"And the lord of Agrigano,
"And the ruler of Armoura,
"Joy to raise the golden eagles
"Of the kingly Leonarchon."

Thus the Prince, with seeming courage,
Knew to hide his coward feelings,
Knew with smoothly ordered language,
To delight the Monarch's hearing.
    Thus the four in secret conclave,
Careless planned of blood and vengeance,
Thus they sat with thoughts unholy,
Warring with the people's freedom,
Till the ghostly hour of midnight
Saw their shrouded figures gliding
'Neath the darkly shadowing columns
Of the dim deserted Temple.

PYLOS.

XIV.

The Fleets sail up the Eurotas.—The Isles-
men join the Armies of Ardoc in the Attack
of Pylos.—The brave defence of the Fortress.
—Anselmo attempts the Passage of the
River, his Vessel is crushed by a falling
Fragment, and the young Hero slain.—The
Fall of Leascar, and Retreat of the Besiegers.
—Gonsalvo's sorrow.— Depression of the
Islesmen.

XIV.

PYLOS.

Swift the squadron of Islanda
Sweeps before the favoring breezes,
Moving on in rapid courses
Up the current of Eurotas.
Sparkling waves of gold and amber
Dash around in playful antics,
As the fleet, with martial music,
Glides along the mighty river.
　All around the changing prospect
Glowed with varied charms before them,
When the morning shed its brightness
From the golden eastern portal,
When the sun's meridian splendour
Poured redundant glory o'er it,
Or when gently fading twilight
Tinged it with its depths of purple.

Groves of feathery palm trees waving,
Traced their broidery on the moonlight;
Lofty woods of hoary pine trees
Rose above the flowing waters;
Fairy gardens spread their fragrance
From the jewelry of their flowers,
Golden fruits in rich profusion,
Hung luxuriant o'er the river;
Stately piles of marble beauty

Smiled upon its shores of emerald;
Terraced walks adorned with sculpture
Led along its banks of verdure;
Sylvan fanes embowered in forests
Shed a sacred calm around them,
While the domes of peopled cities,
Swelling o'er arcades of columns,
O'er long porticoes of granite,
Rose above the playful billows.

Yet at times the changing landscape,
Showed the wilder scenes of nature,
Rugged hills in craggy steepness,
Beetling o'er the lonely hamlet,
Or displayed the great Eurotas,
Spreading out a placid mirror,
Smiling with the gay reflection
Of her hundred flowery Islets.
Mighty stream whose strength meandered
Through the plains of violet verdure,
That resounded with the lowing
Of her countless herds of cattle.

Foamy rills of ivory whiteness,
Warbling brooks of sparkling crystal,
Darker floods of ebon blackness
Sweeping from the distant mountains,
Swelled the fulness of its waters;
While the nobler flowing torrents,
Dashing on through fairy archways,
Darting on o'er rocky barriers,
Flung the thunder of their falling
Far along the peaceful valleys.

Thus the fleet in gliding swiftness
Passed before the awe-struck people,
Thus it swept along Eurotas,
Till the radiance of Aurora

Glowed behind the hills of Pylos;
Till she showed the arrowy river
Surging 'neath the granite mountains,
Showed the heaven-aspiring fortress,
Darkly grand amidst the sunbeams.
There it lay beside Eurotas,
Like a stately crouching lion,
Battled walls and donjon towers,
Lofty bulwarks, frowning ramparts,
Rose before the astonished Islesmen!
  But the swiftly moving vessels,
As they bear them nearer, nearer,
Show the forms of huge balistæ,
Ranging all along the summit;
Misty forms of wonderous engines,
Built to guard the narrow passage,
Built to hurl unmeasured fragments
On the hostile masts beneath them.
And they saw a stately army
Camped around the frowning castle,—
Saw the rising sun illumine
One by one its lofty standards;
Till it tinged the Raven banner,
Floating proudly on the breezes;
Till it blazed upon the ensign
Of the generous sons of Ardoc.
  Now Gonsalvo lands his forces,—
Lands Zorayda's mystic warriors;
Now Leascar, moving downwards,
Hastes to meet Islanda's heroes,
And their rising shouts of greeting,
Tell the friendship of the armies.

But that day the sun in sorrow,
Hid his face in purple tempests,
As he saw the war tried legions

Gleam beneath the rampired fortress,
As the glory thirsting veterans
Rolled their darkling lines upon it ;
As Anselmo's rapid vessels
Poured their clouds of murky vapours
Down the deep flood of Eurotas.

Amalyrac ! then thy waters
First resounded with the roaring
Of the loudly booming cannon.
Then thy lake of purest azure
First re-echoed to the thunder
Of the war-cry of Zorayda,
Then the guardian ranks of Pylos,
Thronging to defend her towers,
Glittered like the Southern Morning,
Rising o'er Antarctic mountains,
As their lances, streaming upward,
Flashed above her battled bulwarks.
    Then along the bright Eurotas
Rose the cries of war and tumult ;
Then her peaceful floods arising,
Writhed beneath the showering granite,
Then the groves of tall acacias
Trembled at the hail of iron,
And the red avenging lightnings
Scared the verdant meads around them.
Then the never shaken bulwarks,
Built by demigods and heroes,
Reeled and crumbled, crashing downwards,
Shedding cataracts of ruins.
And the valleys rocked with terror
When Islanda's darkling columns,
Careless of the blazing firebrands,
Careless of the falling missiles,
Careless of the molten torrents,

Poured in flaming floods upon them.
Marched upon the battered ramparts
Of the tower-encircled Pylos.
   Ranks of escalading warriors,
Planted firm the assailing ladders,
Ardent sons of stately Ardoc,
Shielded by their shadowing bucklers,
Swarmed around her lofty gateways ;
Stern Zorayda's angry rockets
Fell among the huge balistæ.
   Yet the lordly hosts within her,
Guarded well her ruined bastions,
As they hurled assaulting forces
Down into the girdling waters ;
As the sudden opening portals
Poured their legions to the sally,
And their vast machines of warfare
Wracked with whelming rocks Eurotas.

Vainly did the young Anselmo
Dare the gloomy paths of waters,
Vainly had Cruzatlan's seamen
Dauntless braved its thousand terrors.
Yet again their noble leader
Cheered them on amidst the dangers,
And again the fleet of Island
Swept beneath the crags of Pylos.
But the cruel fates arising,
Cut the golden thread of triumph,
. And a storm of crashing ruins
Fell upon Anselmo's vessel ;
All around in scattered splinters,
Dart her towering masts and rigging,
And a dismal cry of horror
Rose around her shattered bulwarks,
As the following ships beheld her

Sinking 'neath the surging water,
Saw the form of young Anselmo
Floating on the blood-stained billows.

But that dismal cry of anguish,
Rising o'er the din of battle,
Reached the army of Leascar,
Reached the forces of Gonsalvo ;
Then their wearied legions gasping,
Maddened at the hero's slaughter,
Rushed with unresisted fury
On the titan towered city.
   Over ruins, over bastions,
Rolls the tempest of their vengeance,
Till the outer walls of Pylos
Bow before Islanda's banner,
Till the exulting troops behold it
Floating on the gory ramparts,
Till the sons of Amalyrac
Flying back, regain the shelter
Of the crag defended castle.
   Yet ! alas ! a faded glory
Was that fleeting hour of triumph,
For the people-blessed Leascar
Lies among the shattered ruins.
Darkening shades of shrouded evening
Checked the long protracted struggle ;
And the mournful sons of Ardoc,
Slow retiring, bore their ruler,
Midst the sounds of lamentation,
From that direful field of conflict.

Then Gonsalvo, sad and weary,
Led his Islesmen to the vessels—
Ah ! no more the young Anselmo's—
For he knew how coming forces,

Thronging from the great Orontes,
Lay beneath the stately temples
Of the ancient Almodira.
And he saw how vain the daring,
Thus repelled and spent with battle,
To again assail the fortress.

Sad and weary was Gonsalvo,
As he gazed in mournful silence
On the calm and marbled features
Of his loved and honored comrade ;
As he saw the young Anselmo,
Saw the lordliest son of Island
Lie a senseless corpse before him.
    Weary was the noble hero—
Weary with the lengthened struggle,
For upon that day of sorrow,
He had wrought heroic wonders ;
He had made the foemen tremble
As they saw his white pluming waving,
As they saw his brandished sabre
Cheering on Zorayda's warriors.
When they saw the black Arabia
Bear his master through the combat.
    But he too, the generous charger,
Had been parted from the hero,
As he foremost scaled the rampart,
Planted there the starry standard,
And was now, midst shouts of triumph,
Led along Eurotas' borders,
Doomed by the exulting captors,
As an offering to the Godhead.
    All alone, the lordly leader
Stood beside Anselmo's body,
Mourning o'er the brave departed,
Mourning o'er the changing fortune

That had dimmed the brightening future,
Seared the hopes that he had fostered,
That the Heavens might yet decree him
To again behold Alonzo.
For he knew the second sunrise
Rose upon the direful combat,
Knew that then the mystic number,
Mystic fifty would be ended.

Dank and drear the night arising,
Spread a dismal darkness o'er him,
Darker still against the flaming
Of the fiery beacon summits,
Lit to spread the news of triumph
To the great imperial city.
Far along the echoing river
Rose the loud victorious shouting
Of the victor hosts of Pylos,
As the vanquished army slowly
Passed into the shrouded distance.

    Down the dark stream of Eurotas,
'Neath the canopy of darkness,
Moved the shattered Islesman vessels.

But a heavier weight of sorrow
Hung impending o'er the heroes,
And disaster, snake enrobed,
Wound her coils still closer round them.
Hark! a voice of mournful boding
Pierces through the gloomy stillness,
But the rising of the night wind
Drowns its accents in its moaning,
Yet the faintly struggling moonbeams
Show a rider spurring onward,
Dashing downwards to the river,
Heated, panting, and dishevelled.

Scarce he waits the range of speaking,
Ere again his broken accents
Sound across the darkened water.
"Fellow comrades, I have brought you
"Anxious tidings from Lorana ;
"There I saw the wearied army
"Of the vanquished Amphilonin.
"For the guards of Amalyrac,
"Leonarchon's chosen veterans,
"Led by the imperial Princes,
"Overpowered the chief in battle.
"And they march by domed Lola,
"On Sargano's fenceless fortress."

Then the veil of consternation
Sunk upon Islanda's warriors ;
Then despair and dark despondence
Spread their sombre shield above them,
For irrevocable fortune
Seemed for ever to pursue them,
Seemed for ever to arrest them,
As they trod the path of glory.
But as the mysterious shadow
Cast at seasons o'er the Daystar,
Circles round itself the glories,
Sprung Eternal from the Godhead ;
So the blasting gloom of sorrow
Rolled upon the lone Gonsalvo,
Borrowed grandeur from the greatness
Of the calm enduring hero,
As he bowed in trustful reverence
To the wise decrees of Heaven.

THE COLISEUM.

XV.

XV.

THE COLISEUM.

Now at length the winged hours
Hasten on the time appointed ;
Now at length the mystic number—
Mystic fifty is accomplished ;
And the seraph sons of Heaven,
Spreading wide their snow-white pinions,
Fly to ope the shadowy portals
That at night enveil the wonders
Of the Daystar's fiery chariot.
　Scarcely had their angel fingers
Touched the bolts of glowing silver,
Ere the cloudy gates retiring,
Turn upon their bronzèd hinges,
And display the glorious beaming
Of the orb that bears the Daystar
Through the maze of universes ;
Of the orb that daily rising
O'er the bastions of Heaven,
Sheds around the bright reflection
Of the ever radiant Godhead ;
For the feeble eyes of mortals
Cannot view the pure resplendence
Of the offspring of the Unknown ;
Cannot view the Power celestial,
Who controls the hosts immortal.

Glorious is that car of wonder,
Shedding flaming beams around it,
Wingéd wheels of living fire
Bear it o'er the paths of ether;
Mighty pinions, self progressing,
Spread afar their four-fold grandeur,
As they slowly move in splendour
Through the boundless constellations :
Dimly shadowed forth to mortals
In a cone of roseate fire,
As their plumes of folded sunlight
Rise amidst the calm of evening,
O'er the slowly sinking Daystar.

Now the dawn's increasing radiance
Tinges all the eastern Heavens,
As the chariot, gliding onwards,
Sheds the dewy showers of blessing
O'er the silent zones beneath it :
As the wheels of living fire
Rest within the vast enclosure
Of the Empyrean palace.
  Then from all the sons of glory
Thronging all her crystal bulwarks,
From the armies of the heroes
Moving o'er the sapphire pavement,
From the starry hosts of Heaven
Ranged along the paths of brightness,
Rose the sweet symphonious music
Of their morning adoration.
  Then the strains of countless lyres
Swelled the long melodious cadence,
Till the ecstasy of pleasure,
Rolling on in waves of rapture,
Bade the diamond domes re-echo
To the chorus of their praises ;

Till the harmonies celestial,
Flowing through the flaming portals,
Fill the thousand halls of sapphire—
Tremble 'neath the fiery towers—
Play among the ruby columns
Wreathed with Amaranthine flowers—
Linger round the rainbow fountains—
Round the springs of endless being ;
Till the sounds with faltering reverence
Enter o'er the solemn threshold—
Through the gates of living fire,—
Enter to the awful presence
Of the ever glorious Daystar ;
Where in splendour unconceivéd,
In the blaze of full refulgence
Rests the Heaven delighting Godhead ;
Where ·he holds the wonderous converse
With the great Unknown, his Father.

O'er him hung the dismal shadow
Of the Spirit of the Midnight,
By him rose the giant terrors
Of the Father of Destruction,
While above the domed vastness
Shone the glory of the Unknown.

For the Gods, in solemn conclave,
Met to rule the fates of Empires,
And that hour had sealed the future
Of the queenly Amalyrac—
Sealed the fortunes of Alonzo—
Of the lordly Leonarchon,
And the dread unchangéd mandate,
Had gone forth to be fulfilléd.

Purely sweet the reverent music
Of the choral adoration,
Swelling through the courts eternal,

Told of the approaching morning.
Then the Spirit of the Midnight
Shrunk into his caves of darkness,
Then the carnage-loving Wargod
Hasted down to blood and slaughter;
But the fair seraphic semblance
Of the ever glorious Daystar
Glides along the trembling palace.
As he moves, the gates of fire
Ope before the awful presence;
And the countless hosts of Heaven,
Bowing down in adoration,
Cast their coronals of starlight
On the pure translucent pavement.
Yet before his sovereign footstep
Treads the fiery wingéd chariot,
Lo! his warning hand prophetic,
Raised afar, displays the terrors
Of his redly flaming falchion;—
Of the sword whose lurid gleaming
Shadows forth the woes of nations.
All the Empires stretched beneath it
Paled before the awful symbol,
As it blazed in deadliest brightness
O'er the fanes of Amalyrac—
O'er the gilded roofs and spires
Of the proud imperial palace,
Filling all her crowded people
With a boding fear of evil
As they gazed upon the crimson
Of its blade of flaming redness;
As they saw its glare reflected
On the waves of the Eurotas.

Yet not long the Power eternal
Held on high the sign of terror,

Slow he sheathed the blazing portent,
And assumed the golden lyre,
To whose notes the Hosts of Heaven
Sweep along in mystic dances.

Now he mounts the living chariot,
Trembling at the present Godhead,
And the harp's celestial music
Leads along the sons of glory.
Grandly from the courts of azure
Rose the wingèd orb's resplendence,
Pouring beams of dazzling daylight,
Tempered with the clouds of blessing,
O'er the Adamautine bulwarks
Of the Empyrean city :
Till they tinged the towery grandeur
Of the Daystar's acient temple,
Spreading forth their genial influence
O'er the beauties of creation.

Then the eye of the all-seeing,
In the fulness of refulgence,
Rested on his own loved city,
On the queenly Amalyrac.
Through her gates the thronging nations
Crowd to see the wonderous combat.
All along her streets of columns
Pour the multitudes of people,
Surging upward to the summit,
Where the Coliseum's grandeur
Rears its tenfold rows of arches,
Rears its tower-encircled precincts ;
Casting wide a mighty shadow
O'er the lakes' cerulean water.
But though awe o'ercame the stranger,
As he viewed the vast exterior,
Wonder filled his throbbing bosom

When he scaled the lofty turrets,
As he saw the crowding nations
Rolling like a living ocean
Through her hundred giant porches,
As he marked the lengthened ranges
Of her festive seats of marble
Rising tier on tier around him ;
Saw a myriad snow-white columns
Hung with gold embroidered drapery,
Bearing up the graven friezes,—
Bearing up the polished brightness
Of her balustrades of beauty,
Gay with veins of varied colour,
Graced with wreaths of odorous flowers.

Glancing up, the eye bewildered,
Climbed the rows of circling couches,
Till it saw the reddening richness
Of the topmost range of arches
Traced against the clear refulgence
Of the azure vaults of Heaven.
In the centre, broad extended,
Lay the sand bestrewn arena,
Where the sons of Amalyrac
Wont to strive in manly daring.

Circling round it stood the legions
Of the warriors of Orontes,
With their gaily floating banners,
With their lances gleaming brightly—
Guardians of her stately portals.

Save along the southern barrier
Where the famed Epiromenes,
With the veterans of his army—
All the troops of Epidaurus—
Held the foremost post of honor
At the great imperial entrance.

To the northward on his chariot,
Close beneath the imperial shadow
Of the throne of Leonarchon
Stood the ruler of Orontes.
High above in solemn grandeur,
In their richly broidered vestures
Sat the Hierarch of the Wargod—
Sat the High Priest of the Daystar;
While between, in calm composure,
Robéd in the sacred garments,
Rests the mighty sovereign Pontiff,
Rests the High Priest of the Unknown.
To the right hand, to the left hand,
Stretch the colleges of learning;
While beneath, arrayed in order,
Wait the ivory thrones preparéd
For the rulers of the people.

But the destined hour approaches,
And the spacious pile is crowded
With the nations of the Empire—
With the beauty of her daughters—
With the prime of all her manhood,
With the wisdom of her sages.
Youth and age alike impatient,
Line the balconies of marble;
Haughty kings and lordly princes
Fill her stately seats of honor;
Subject kingdoms, mighty cities,
Pour their sons to view the combat.

From the crowded streets and causeways
Of the ancient Almodira:
From the looms of golden tissue
'Neath the domes of Megalasca;
From the dark and cloudy regions

Of the coal producing Carzan ;
From the lurid midnight redness
Of the flaming springs of Jerah ;
From the land where lonely Sephar
Sees the sun's meridian brightness
Blazing o'er the peaks of Ardoc ;
From the province of Armoura,
Bordering on Alloria's kingdoms ;
From the palaced pride of Oro,
Frowning o'er the inland ocean ;
From the Islands of Zaurana,
Rich with mines of gold and silver ;
From the bright and happy kingdom
Of the Queen of Epidaurus ;
From the deep and solemn stillness
Of Dolona's ancient temples,
Where the heaven delighting Daystar
First beheld his father's glory ;
From the lake whose placid beauty
Sees the forests of Phoccia
Waving o'er the "Diamond Mountain ; "
From the woody land of Lara,
Where the broad stream of Eurotas
First beholds the Empire's borders ;
From the rich metallic passes
Leading to the far Ancyra ;
From the wide and fertile champaign
Of the plains of Agrigano,
Whose Pelasgic towers in wonder
View the awe-inspiring vastness
Of the peaks of Zon Sorado—
Of the long gigantic outline
Of the mighty southern mountains
That defend the sacred empire
From the icy rage of winter,
Whose eternal, changeless summits,

Veiled in snow from everlasting,
Look in calm unbroken silence
On the ever restless ocean—
On the isles of floating crystal,
Moving o'er the azure water,
On the full luxuriant verdure
Of the kingdoms of Orontes—
    From the nations, who rejoicing,
First behold the orient Daystar,
To the people, who in sorrow,
Watch his eve-departing splendour,
From the whole extended greatness
Of the realms of Amalyrae—
Came that rich and crowding concourse
To behold the mystic challenge ;
For the fame of Xiloe's conqueror
Spread afar to distant regions,
And the wondering people hailed him
As the offspring of the Daystar.

Now the sounds of solemn music
Tell of the approaching pageant,
And the crimson robéd heralds
Loud proclaim the coming Monarch,
Low the troops of Epidaurus
Bend to earth their gleaming ensigns,
As the blazoned eagle banner
Soars beneath the giant portal.
    And the legions of Orontes
Hail with shouts the gorgeous standard,
As it floats beneath the shadow
Of the Coliseum's vastness—
As it leads the long procession
O'er the wide outstretched arena.
In its pathway youths and maidens
Strew the ground with odorous flowers,

While the martial ranks of music
Follow, each in destined order.
  Till before that great assembly
Moved the high commanding figure
Of the King, whose haughty sceptre
Sways the regions of Phoceia ;
Who enrobed in regal vestments,
Glittering midst his subject princes,
Bears on high the imperial radiance
Of the crown of Amalyrac,
Proudly bears the gleaming brightness
Of the diadem of power—
Of the ancient jewelled circlet
That had shone upon the forehead
Of a hundred mighty monarchs,
That had blazed in beams celestial
On the brows of old Almodad ;
When the everlasting Daystar
In the dimness of Dolona
Gave it to the generous offspring
Of his war-delighting brother,
And commanded him to keep it,
And to charge his sons and daughters
That they wield the sceptre lightly,
Lest a day of retribution
Hasten on the destined hour ;
Lest their Empire be o'erwhelmed
Ere the time before appointed.

Still the long line of procession
Sweeps before in stately measure,
Till the lordly Leonarchon
Treads the stairs of polished marble,
Till he mounts the throne of ivory
That had seen him first invested
With the emblems of his power.

In his hand the emerald sceptre,
Glitters in the glancing sunbeams,
And the gems of his tiara
Gleam upon his noble forehead.
Now his haughty eye majestic,
Ranges o'er the vast assembly,
And a flush of conscious power
Glows across his manly features,
As he sees arrayed before him
All the glory of his Empire;
Sees his proud aspiring wishes
Hastening to a sure fulfilment;
As he muses on the tidings
Brought him on that welcome morning,
Of Lorana's field of triumph,
Of the fall of great Leascar,
Vanquished 'neath victorious Pylos.
As he knew no common mortal
Could maintain the unequal struggle,
Doomed upon the stranger warrior;
For he feared the mystic fable
Of the Sun's avenging offspring,
And he longed to see the hour
Fatal to the great Alonzo.

Still the long line of procession
Sweeps before in stately measure;
Here the Empress Cleopatra
Moves amidst her robes of ermine;
Here the Empire's maiden daughters
Glide along in youthful beauty.
First the tall and graceful Hera
Emulates her queenly mother,
With her veil of golden tissue
Flashing back the rays of sunlight;
Then Chrysothemis, the lovely,

Leaning on the fair Irene,
Scarcely daring to look upward
At the multitudes around her.

Then the King of Old Dolona
Sprung from Cleopatra's father ;
Foremost in the rank of princes—
Basking in imperial favour ;
Then the kinsmen of the Monarch,
Then the train of ancient sages ;
Till before that great assembly
Glides the long imposing order
Of the solemn priestly systrum.
In whose centre, high upraiséd,
Borne upon its couch of crimson,
Beamed the brightly polished splendour
Of the sacred sword Phlegathron.
As they pass, an awful silence
Spreads around the thronging nations,
And the chorus of their voices
Rises o'er the death-like stillness.

CHORUS.

Who shall be able to wield the great falchion ?
Who shall be able to bear it in battle ?
None but the Brother of the red Wargod—
None but the Offspring of the bright Daystar.

See ye its hilt, one diamond of beauty,
Plucked from the gardens of Heaven in its glory ;
See ye its blade all radiant with sunbeams,
Wrought in the caves of the Spirit of Midnight.

So it beamed bright in the hand of the Godhead,
Beamed in the hand of the Father of Sunlight,
As the huge form of the Giant of Ouran
Fell like a meteor, shaking the planets.

And when the terrible Spirit of Darkness
Sought to enveil the world with its horrors,
Then at the sight of its blazing refulgence,
Fled the vast shade to the caverns of ocean.

But it now sleeps the long slumber of ages,
Resting in silence the symbol of power,
Waiting the season, all dimly foreshadowed—
When it shall wake to the thunder of battle.

Rise then, ye Nations, rise and adore it !
Rise and adore it, the symbol of Power !
None shall e'er wield it, but the bright Daystar,
None shall e'er bear it, but his great Offspring,
Rise then, ye Nations, rise and adore it,
Rise and adore the symbol of Power.

Then the whole of that assembly,
Filled with awe and reverent feelings,
Rose before the sacred falchion ;
While the priests in mystic order,
Placed it by the crown of Empire—
Placed it on the ancient altar,
Built beneath the solemn shadow
Of the throne of Amalyrac.

Still the long line of procession
Sweeps before in stately measure,
Till the sons of Epidaurus

Hail their loved imperial mistress,
Raising loud the clang of armour,
As they strike their burnished bucklers.

Till the eyes of the assembly
Rest upon her lovely daughter—
On the peerless form of beauty,
On the star of Amalyrac.
From her coronal of crystal
Fell the envious veil that ever
Hid her fair and perfect features
From the vision of the people:
For the haughty Leonarchon
Feared the power of her enchantment.
But in vain the cruel Monarch,
Sought to hide it from the nation;
For the mystery shed o'er her,
And her graceful, queenly bearing—
As she moved in robes of whiteness,
Girdled with a band of jewels—
Spread a holy charm around her,
Made her seem some purer being
Nurtured in the courts of Heaven.

Long and loud had been the greeting
That received the lordly Monarch,
As he passed in kingly pageant
Through the giant Coliseum.
Yet a fuller voice of welcome
Hailed the entrance of the Princess,
Thrilling through the envious spirit
Of the Master of the Eagle.
Now in rich and gorgeous vestures
Sweeps along the Queen of Oro.
Here is seen the dark eyed beauty
Of the daughter of Zourana;
Here the proud commanding glances
Of the sovereign of Eurotas

Brooding o'er palatial cities
In the power of Island's armies.
Here the Princess of Ancyra,
With her rich and golden tresses,
Who had left her father's towers,
Frowning o'er the wild Phialla;
Gazing on the forms gigantic,
On the grandest works of Nature;
Gazing on the snow-clad mountains
Rising in aspiring vastness
Straight above the lake's dark water
Closing in its awful wildness
With their Heaven assaulting summits;
Gazing on the wonderous vision
Of the falls of the Phoceia;
Where the broad and foaming river,
Thundering far along the valley,—
Roaring through the riven chasm—
Leaps a thousand cubits downward,
Hurling its stupendous torrent
To the stillness of Phialla.

Here is seen the haughty sister
Of the Monarch of Sargano,
Who beheld the sons of Ardoc
Ruling in his stately palace.
Here the lord of Araxeia,
Here the chief of Ismanutha,
Here the ever frowning features
Of the tyrant of Armoura.

Still the long line of procession
Sweeps before in stately measure.
Now enrobed in purple garments,
Move the envoys of the kingdoms;
Move the ambassadors and princes

From the mighty neighbouring Empires,
From the distant Realms and Nations
Throned upon the boundless ocean.

First the haughty Lord of Manca
Shadows forth Alloria's greatness,
Shadows forth the gay profusion
Of his lord's barbaric splendour ;
Of the King, whose yoke of iron
Weighed upon the fertile Mora,
Of the King, whose dark ambition,
Raged along the hills of Ardoc,
And insatiate, poured his terrors
O'er the groves of Parasmana.
Here the chieftain of Lodargo,
From Mediro's mountain valleys,
Spread beneath the sacred shadow
Of Dolona's snow-clad summits.
Here are seen the stately legates
Of the powerful western kingdoms ;
From the dark embattled grandeur
Of Chrysaor's sea-girt borders ;
From the vales of Ironama,
Sinking to the stormy ocean,
Crownéd with the ruggéd outline
Of Dinorma's misty Islands ;
From the fairy Almanula,
From the land of smiling waters,
Far behind the solemn valleys,
Where the Oracle of Wisdom
Tells the destinies of nations ;
From the hills of Constellara,
From the kingdoms of Moskella,
From the golden fields that glitter
O'er the queenly land of Leila.
Each had sent its noblest princes
To the great imperial city ;

Each had sent its lordliest envoy
To the Court of Amalyrac.

Still the long line of procession
Sweeps before in stately measure,
Till the Ruler of the city,
In the pride of civic honor ;
Till her Senators of wisdom,
In their sable robes of office,
Close the grand imposing semblance
Of the power of Amalyrac.

THE CHALLENGE.

XVI.

Leonarchon summons Alonzo, who enters
in the Arms of Philolaos — The High
Priest of the Unknown warns Leonarchon
to stay the Challenge.—He, unheeding, bids
them unloose the Eagle. — Alonzo over-
comes in the first three Combats, but has
only a Broken Sword to defend him from
the Giants.—Yet he slays the first : when the
Entrance of Arabia checks the Advance of
the others.—Alonzo, Master of the Bolts
of Thunder, obtains the Victory.

XVI.

THE CHALLENGE.

Now the Nations of the Empire
Resting on their seats of marble,
Wait with scarce restrained impatience
For the coming of the hero.
  Thrice ten myriad eyes are turnéd
Towards the lordly Leonarchon,
Eager for the appointed summons
That shall call the wonderous warrior
To the great unequal combat.

Lo ! the offspring of Almodad,
Rising from his throne of ivory,
Stretches forth the emerald sceptre
Towards the ancient granite Altar ;
And his accents, clear and stately,
Sounding through the Coliseum,
Reach the famed Epiromenes :
" Bring the stranger Champion forward ! "

All the multitudes were silent,
Bending down in expectation,
As they gazed in anxious longing
On the high imperial entrance.
  Now the troops of Epidaurus
Seem to turn in still amazement ;

Now the legions of Orontes
Waver backward, filled with wonder,
And the lance of car-borne Oro
Quivers with its master's terrors.

Now a cold and deadly pallor
Creeps o'er Leonarchon's visage,
As he sees Epiromenes
Enter with the stranger Champion ;
And the eager expectation
Of the nations of the Empire
Changes too to thrilling wonder
As they gaze upon the figure—
On the armour of the hero.

Till when words and faltering whispers
First gave utterance to their feelings,
" Philolaos !   Philolaos ! "
Rose from all their countless thousands,
" Philolaos !   Philolaos ! "
Rang around the mighty precincts ;
For they see the white plume waving
O'er the crown-encircled helmet ;
See the semblance of the Daystar
Flaming on the golden buckler ;
Know the ruby handled falchion
That had led them on to triumph ;
And the figure of Alonzo,
As he trod the wide arena,
Brought to mind the great departed,
In his days of youthful valour,
When the Gonfanon of Xiloe
Waved above the Empire's armies.

But the leader of Islanda
Moved with a yet statelier bearing,
And from 'neath his kingly forehead
Darted forth a fiercer fire,
And his countenance seemed beaming

With a still more godlike presence.
But a flush of deeper feeling
Seems to tinge the warrior's features,
As his eye, in darting swiftness,
Ranges o'er the thronéd powers ;
As it rests in lingering rapture
On the Heavenly Amarantha.
Even she, the lovely Princess,
Started when she saw Alonzo
In the panoplied resplendence
Of her long lamented father ;
And a tear of sad remembrance
Glistened in her eyes of azure,
As he seemed to stand before her
In the pride of youthful ardour.
Oh ! how welcome was the covering
Of her veil's embroidered tissue,
As she felt the rising blushes
Answering to the frowning glances
Cast upon her by the Monarch.
For he knew that none could glitter
In the arms of Philolaos,
Ere he had obtained the favor
Of his fair and queenly daughter.

Then the multitudes of people,
Rousing from their deep amazement,
Saw how the imperial helmet
Gleamed upon the stranger Champion,
And they shuddered at the daring
That had led the great adventurer
Thus to gather hopeless dangers
Round the terrors of the combat.
For they knew that he who blazéd
In the arms of Philolaos,
Stood revealed the stern accuser

'Of the mighty Leonarchon,
And arraigned the haughty Monarch
As usurper of the kingdom ;
Then their sympathy arising,
Thought of all the days of blessing,
When the Father of his people
Led them on the paths of triumph ;
Thought how all the Northern nations
Rose against their despot ruler—
Thought of all the pride and glory
Of an Empress Amarantha.

But meanwhile the arméd warrior
Strides the Coliseum's vastness.
As he moves, the noon-day radiance
Blazes on the diamond umbo,
And his cuirass, gemmed with jewels,
Flashes back the streams of sunlight ;
Till he seems indeed the Offspring
Of the ever beaming Daystar.
Proud he moves, till at the centre
Of the wide outstretched arena :
Stern he rears his steely javelin,
Resting on his burnished buckler,
And his lordly voice arises
Clear amidst the gathering stillness :
"Mighty King of Amalyrac !
"I demand the lawful Challenge—
"I demand the mystic Challenge
"With the Elements of Nature."

Then the High Priest of the Unknown,
Rising with the sacred college,
Spake in slow and solemn measure :
"Monarch ! Kings ! and wealthy nations
"Of the realms of Amalyrac !

" Lo ! the mystic time appointed
" By the oracle of Wisdom,
" Has fulfilled its destined courses.
" And thy voice, O ! Leonarchon,
" Now alone can free the Champion.
" Hearken to my words, I pray thee,
" Ere the changeless fate be spoken ;
" For the dreadly flaming falchion
" Of the ever glorious Daystar,
" That dire portent that foreboding
" Tells of woes and coming slaughter,
" Blazed this morn in lurid redness
" O'er the great imperial palace,
" Gleamed in crimson rays of bloodshed
" O'er the waves of the Enrotas.
" I beheld it, and its meaning
" Shone before my agéd eyesight,
" I beheld it, but I may not
" Tell the omen to the people ;
" But do thou, O ! mighty Monarch,
" Hear the ancient Pontiff's counsel,
" Weigh the words of timely warning,
" While I charge thee, Leonarchon,
" That thou stay the mystic Challenge."

Thus he spake, and for a season
Hope o'erspread the great assembly,
Till the ruler of the Empire,
Frowning towards the reverend Pontiff,
Bids them not delay the combat,
Bids them loose the warrior Eagle.
Then the solemn priestly systrum,
Circling round the ancient altar,
Raised the chorus of their voices,
Sounding o'er the tiers of marble.

CHORUS.

Bring forth the Eagle—the First of Creation,
Bring forth the Storm-bird, the Lord of the
　　Mountain,
Born on the whirlwind, cradled in tempests,
　　　　Emblem of Ether.

When the dark world is rolling in thunder,
When the red lightning is darting around it,
Then he soars calm in the azure of Heaven,
　　　　Gleaming in Sunlight.

For he has founded his palace of crystal,
High on the fanes of the mighty Sorardo,
Where he sits throned on the snows everlasting,
　　　　Gazing on Heaven.

Bring forth the Storm-bird, Sovereign of combat,
Lord of the air and emblem of Ether !
He who o'ercomes him, hurls at his footstool
　　　　Nature's first Power.

As they ceased, a pluméd shadow
Sweeps along the great arena,
And the nations, gazing upwards,
See the golden-pinioned eagle
Soaring high above the towers ;
Poised in air, now o'er the people,
Hovering now above the helmet
Of the ruler of Islanda—
So he hovered o'er his quarry
In his own majestic valleys,

Where the sources of Orontes,
Pouring from the icy portal—
From the clear cerulean archway,
Roll their dark and gloomy waters
Through the dread impending chasms;
Through the huge unmeasured vastness
Of the overshadowing mountains;
Through their bastions of granite
Crowned with never ending winter.

But no more the powerful pinions
Of the bird of Leonarchon,
Rest all motionless in ether:
See he stoops, and swooping downwards,
Darts upon the crested hero,
Like the shaft of vivid fire,
That descending from its palace
In the wracking clouds of Heaven,
Falls upon a lonely column,
Sole memorial of its city.
Yet as still, the sage's wisdom,
Knows to stay the threatening ruin,
So Alonzo, calm and stately,
Watched, unawed, the mighty eagle.
High he raised his beamy javelin,
Bending back his godlike figure—
Waiting for the coming danger.
Dark he sees the shade above him,
Hears the whistling of its pinions,
And with firmly guiding power,
Hurls the swift ascending weapon.

Then a chill of anxious boding
Crept through Amarantha's bosom,
And her eyes, with dimness shaded,

Saw no more the great Alonzo.
But the sound of shouting people,
Echoing o'er the Coliseum,
Broke the mazy spell that bound her,
And she saw the helméd Champion,
Scatheless from the primal contest,
Draw the death-directed javelin
From the lifeless form before him.
Gloomy scowls of indignation
Darkened Leonarchon's forehead,
As he saw the Lord of Ether,
In whose strength he viewed the emblem
Of his own imperial greatness,
Fall so soon before the hero ;
And his sovereign voice arising,
Hastens on the hoped-for vengeance,
As he gives the mighty mandate
For the second deadly combat.

Then again the priestly systrum,
Robéd in their sacred garments,
Raised the chorus of their voices,
Sounding o'er the wide arena.

CHORUS.

Bring forth the Alligator,
  Ranger of Rivers,
Bring forth the dreaded beast,
  Terror of Nations.
Slow he moves onward
  In grandeur and silence,
Gliding along
  In the glory of Power.

See him arrayèd
  In adamantine armour,
See his red eyeballs
  Irradiate with fury.
Thus he stalks proud on
  The banks of Eurotas,
Thus rules her deep floods,
  Monarch of Waters.

He who shall vanquish him,
  Victor in the combat,
Stands the great Lord
  O'er the powers of the Ocean.
Bring then the dreaded beast,
  Fearful to gaze on,
Bring forth the terror
  Of the children of Lara.

Ere they cease, the giant Lizard,
Moving slowly o'er the arena,
Glided towards the stately Champion ;
Wide he oped his gulphy vastness,
Bristling with serrated terrors,
Shook his tail in rising fury,
Whirled the clouds of dust around him,
And his eyeballs darting fire
View with joy the certain victim.
On he glides, his scaly harness
Rattles as he hastens forward,—
As he sees the great Alonzo
Poising his uplifted javelin :
Brightly gleamed the steely weapon,
While the hero's steady vision,
Aimed it at the Dread of Rivers ;
And it blazed a darting meteor,

As it cleft the fields of Heaven.
Down it falls with force impetuous,
Falls upon the mailéd body;
But the adamantine armour
Hurled the ponderous weapon backward,
Broken, shattered into shivers.
  Then the crowds of anxious people,
Fearing for the lonely warrior—
For the champion of their Princess,
Bent in anxious silence forward.
Still the gliding beast moves onward,
Shrieking in its horrid pleasure;
Till it grasps Islanda's ruler,
Rearing high its scaly breastplate;
Till it holds the kingly hero
In its slimy, cold embraces.
Now its giant tail is wreathéd,
Bending in the golden armour,
Now its ghastly jaws are gaping,
Closing o'er the pluméd helmet.
  Then Alonzo felt endurance
Sinking 'neath the crushing monster,
Then a deeper thrill of terror
Ran through all that great assembly;
Then the haughty Leonarchon
Smiled to see his wish accomplished.
And the Princess Amarantha,
Sunk upon her mother's bosom,
Hid her lovely face in mourning.

But behold the Lord of Island,
Straining all his utmost powers,
Frees his right arm from its bondage,
And a sudden cry of gladness
Sounds around the pillared precincts,
As the ruby falchion flashes

O'er the crown-encircled helmet
Like the sunbeam on a billow,—
As he sheathed the steely azure
'Neath the Alligator's eyebrow,
And the lifeless body sinking,
Fell a mass of helpless ruin,
Making all the great arena,
Trembling answer to its slaughter.

Yet Alonzo, scarce arising,
Freed him from the scaly lizard,
Ere again the solemn priesthood
Woke the measure of their chorus.

CHORUS.

Loose ye the terrible Lion, Lord of the hills of
    Deserta,
Bring forth the Emblem of Earth, Prince of the
    Beasts of the plain.
Woe to the stranger, who heedless, rouses him
    up in his anger,
Woe to the sons of the chase, who shall disturb
    his repose.
Then all the oaks of the forest shake at the
    sound of his roaring,
Then the full voice of his wrath echoes afar
    from his lair ;
But when the shades of the evening tell of the
    coming of midnight,
Then he goes forth in his pride, roaming the
    hills for his prey.
Then he spreads fear o'er the valleys, prowling
    along in the moonbeams,
Showing his mighty shape, dark on the brow of
    the hill.

Yet still fiercer he roves, through the endless
    woods of Phoccia,
And still vaster his form, filling the nations with
    fear ;
Glory to him whose valor, shall tame the pride
    of his anger,
He who shall lay him low, rules o'er the spirits
    of earth.
Loose then the terrible lion, symbol of strength
    and of greatness,
Bring forth the forest king, Lord of the beasts
    of the plain.

But an awful sound rebounding
From the myriad marble columns,
Breaks upon the priestly chorus,
Sending an unwilling shudder
Through the crowd of kings and nations ;
And an anxious thrill of terror
Blanched the dames of Amalyrac
As they saw the tawny monster—
As they viewed the vast proportions
Of Phoccia's fiercest Lion.
On he moves in devious courses,
Seeking his accustomed victim.
Now he glares upon the assembly,
Springing at the circling barriers.
Now at length his glowing eyeballs
Rest upon the great Alonzo,
And a louder roar resounding,
Echoes forth its awful thunder,
As he seems to hail a champion
Worthy of his lordly prowess.
And the Princess Amarantha
Clasped her hands to stay her feelings,

As she watched his mane arising,
Bristling up with gathering fierceness,
As she saw him bounding forward,
Straining all his giant muscles—
Saw him crouching down in silence,
Gazing grimly on Alonzo;
Till she shudders from the vision,
As she hears the direful death-spring.

But the Champion, ever watchful,
Leaps aside with agile swiftness,
And the forest king in fury,
Lashes round his tail in anger,
For he feels the ready warrior,
Wound him with the ruby falchion,
Sees his destined prey uninjured,
Stand in all his pride before him;
Yet again he dashes onward,
And again, with straining ardour,
Springs with fiercer, deadlier raging,
Grappling with Islanda's ruler.
  Then the Princess, lost in horror,
Gazed in fixed and eager anguish,
As she saw her loved Alonzo
Vainly seek to ward the danger,
Heard the ringing plates of armour
Clash upon the great arena,
As she thought she saw the Lion
Rend his mangled form to pieces.

Silence! sad and mournful silence,
Reigned around the Coliseum,
As the nations watched the combat—
As they viewed the unequal struggle—
As they saw the hero wrestling

With the terror of Phoceia.
  Vainly did the golden .buckler
Shield him from the tawny monarch,
For his teeth, with grinding harshness,
Wrenched the burnished plates of armour.
  But a direful howl arising,
Breaks the spell of strained attention—
Ends the joy of Leonarchon.
And Alonzo the victorious,
Wields around his broken falchion,
As he looks with mien triumphant
On the vast and lifeless monster,
Looks upon the gory forehead,
Gleaming with the shivered fragment
Witness of that desperate struggle.
But the never daunted leader
Knew the overpowering effort,—
Felt the feeble hope of conquering,
Thus unarmed and spent and wearied,
All the four-fold strength of giants.
And the lovely Amarantha,
Rousing from her fearful dreaming,
Boded that each fleeting moment
Was the last for her Alonzo.

But again the cruel monarch
Hastens on the direful combat,
And again the priestly systrum
Raise the long and solemn chorus.

CHORUS.

Lo ! their are Fires—above us—beneath us—
Sprung in their forms from the hand of the
    Godhead,
Fires celestial beaming in brightness,

Fires terrestrial—blessing and cursing,
Fires of Midnight—ever destroying,
Fires of Judgment—flaming from Heaven.

Where shall we find the Emblem of Fire ?
Where on the earth ? or where in the water ?
Where in the far stretching fields of the ether ?
Which of the beasts of the dark waving forest ?
Which of the wild birds, that soar o'er the
    mountains ?
Which of the sons of the wide rolling ocean
Boast to resemble the offspring of Heaven ?
None can assume the primal distinction,
None represent the essence of Being.

    Man is the Lord of Creation—
    His spirit the Emblem of Fire ;
    Man, when he walks in his glory,
    Shines like the sun in the zenith ;
    Man, with his changing affections,
    Glows like the flame of a furnace ;
    Man, when he rises in anger,
    Flames like the river of Midnight ;
    Man, when he moves the avenger,
    Strikes like the arrows of Heaven.

Come then, ye Giants, to battle and slaughter,
Come to the awful and mystical combat.

Lo ! they have come from the kingdoms,
The farthest realms of the Empire ;
Come from the mighty shadow !
The snow-clad peaks of Sorardo ;
Come from the northern mountains,
The deep blue hills of Circano ;
Come from the golden isles,

The joy of the ocean of Oro ;
Come from the evening land,
The fertile region of Lara.
He who shall break their power,
Their four-fold strength in the challenge,
Reigns in the realms everlasting,
Lord o'er the powers of Nature.

Come then, ye Giants, to battle and slaughter—
Come to the awful and mystical combat.

As the solemn priestly chorus,
Slow retiring, leave the Altar,
All the eyes of the assembly
Gaze upon the towering figures
Of the chosen sons of Empire,—
Gaze upon their limbs of iron ;
None but raised his armed shoulders
High above Alonzo's helmet.
　By the circling northern bulwark,
'Neath the throne of Leonarchon,
Stood the gloomy crestéd Geiro.
O'er his head, his arms enormous,
Swing his ponderous flail in menace ;
To the south, the huge Diospur
Rests upon his weighty javelin—
On his spear, a single pine tree,
Rooted from the groves of Lara.
Here upon the western circuit—
Moves the giant of Sorardo—
Moves Helion's swarthy figure ;
On his shoulder rest the terrors
Of his boss-embronzéd war-club ;
While beside the Eastern barrier
Rose the form of haughty Thonor ;

He, the tallest of the children,
Of Circano's mountain valleys;
By his side is seen the glitter
Of his axe's whetted sharpness,
On his casque the flaming dragon,
Red with furnace glowing brightness.
Such the foe whose strength gigantic,
Threatens to overwhelm Alonzo,
Such the last and greatest danger,
Dread impending o'er the hero.
And the ruler of Islanda,
As he weighed the hopeless striving,
Felt his ardent spirit failing,—
Felt the shadow of Destruction
Darkening all his hopes of glory.
Then the night of desperation
Soon had wrapt him in its mazes,
Had not undefined feelings
Led his eyes in sorrow upwards
To the beauteous Amarantha,
As their long and lingering glances
Seemed to say "Farewell for ever."
But when he beheld his loved one—
When he saw the veiléd figure
Sinking 'neath her growing anguish,
When he viewed the tyrant glances
Of the frowning Leonarchon,
When he thought of her unaided,
Victim of a direful vengeance—
Burning ardour glowed within him,
Flaming into desperate courage,
And then, Woe! to him whose daring
Leads him in the Champion's pathway.

But not long the boastful Geiro
Waits to join the easy combat.

See he strides along majestic,
Swinging round his flail of iron,
And in mockery prays Alonzo
Not to slay his helpless victim.
    Then the lord of great Islanda
Felt the furies raging in him,—
Then he snatched the broken fragment
Of the sword of Philolaos,
And arousing all his forces,
Flung it fiercely at the boaster.

Wonder filled the Kings and Princes,
As they saw him thus unheeding,
Hurl away his only weapon,—
Hurl away in desperation,
All the hope that chance had given him.
    But a dumb amazement followed,
As the congregated powers
Saw the deeply dented falchion
Strike the giant's bronzéd forehead :
As they saw the haughty Geiro,
Trembling drop the threatening iron,
As they heard his armèd figure
Clanking fall upon the arena.
    Then the great Alonzo, even
Scarcely owned the easy triumph
As he gazed upon the vastness
Of the mail-invested warrior.
    Yet he knew each wingéd moment
Carried fate upon its pinions,
And he hastes to gain the succour
Of Armoura's ponderous weapon.
As he stoops, the giant brethren,
Joining in barbaric laughter,
Vowing vengeance for their comrade,
Rush upon the lonely hero.

But a deeper sound arises
From the spacious outer precincts,
Like the roar of tossing ocean
Rolling to the imperial portal ;
And Alonzo, turning towards it,
Hears it swelling, louder, louder,
Till the stately Coliseum
Echoes back the mighty surging ;
Sees the whole assembly breathless,
All forgetful of his danger,
Wait amazed the coming uproar,
Till the upper ranks of people
Raise a cry of fear and wonder,
Till the three advancing champions
Stand entranced like graven statues.
Onward rolls the approaching tumult,
Pealing in discordant thunder,
E'en the guards of Epidaurus
Seem to shrink unwilling backward ;
Clouds of dust—pursuing people
Fill at once the lofty entrance,
And an undefinéd terror
Spreads o'er all the sons of Empire.
Lordly Oro's gleaming warriors,
Lost to order leave their stations,
Springing o'er the circling barriers
Crowding towards the Northern bulwark;
For they see a gloomy charger
Darting wildly thro' the gateway ;
From his wide distended nostrils
Pours the tempest of his snorting,
From his eyes inflaméd redness
Seems to glow unearthly fire,—
From his bridled mouth in showers
Shoots the white spray of his foaming,
O'er his archéd neck dishevelled

Flies his sable mane disordered,
While his tail in flowing blackness
Streams afar its grim profusion.
On he comes, the sand arising
Rolls like clouds of smoke around him;
On he comes, the maddened courser
Laying low the rash pursuers,
Throwing back the polished roundness
Of his shining hoofs in anger;
In he darts, his sinewy power
Bounds with unrestrainéd swiftness
O'er the far outstretched arena,
Filling all the awe-struck people
With a superstitious terror.
Some exclaimed with trembling accents
"Lo! the Spirit of the Midnight,"
Some affrighted, shrieking, crushing,
Vainly seek to fly the vision.
  Yet he dashes on unheeding,
Charging straight upon Alonzo.

Then the Pontiff of the Daystar,
Stretching forth his ivory sceptre,
Cries aloud above the tumult:
"See the vengeance poured by Heaven,
"On the impious son of slaughter."

But the words were scarcely uttered,
Ere the hero, striding forward,
In the pride of godlike presence,
Laid his hand upon the courser,
Prancing in careering wildness.
  Were they words of hidden magic
That the stranger Champion whispered?
Are they spells of dark enchantment

That have stayed the heavenly vengeance;
See at once the furious war-horse
Checks the thunder of his charging,
And the astonished concourse see him,
Calm and motionless as marble,
Standing by the great Alonzo.

Awed they watch the godlike hero,
Gazing at the well-known courser;
See the steed in conscious safety,
Answer back the fond caresses
That the hope inspired Alonzo
Pours upon the black Arabia.
Yet a sudden thought arising,
Weighed upon his anxious spirit,
Boding of his brother dying,
Lonely on a field of battle.
    And in vain the faithful charger,
Looking whistfully upon him,
Seeks to tell the mournful story
Of the bloody day of Pylos.
How he saw his noble master
Climb the lofty bulwarked vessels;
How the exulting victors dragged him
All along the grassy meadows,
Till the second morning brought them
To the great imperial city;
How he reared and started backwards,
Striving with his wearied captors,
As they urged him on in triumph
Through the granite-paven forum,
All along the streets and causeways,
Up the capitolian roadway;
How at length he battled with them,
Striking down the astonished leaders,

Plunging furious through the people,
Who, affrighted, flying, fainting,
Made a spacious road before him,
Leading to the towery portal
Of the mighty Coliseum.

But again the giant warriors,
Rousing from their trancéd silence,
Thirsting to avenge their comrade—
Move impetuous on Alonzo.
  Swift he hastes the girths to tighten,
Swift he springs into the saddle,
And he sees a ray of promise
Piercing through the gloomy future,
As his kingly eye delighted,
Glancing o'er the stately trappings
Rests upon a sleeping weapon.
  Yet, before Islanda's ruler,
Raised on high the bright revolver—
Threatening shouts, ironic tauntings,
Warn him of a foe approaching.
For the stalworth Thonor following,
Swings his axe with deadly power;
Aiming its unblemished sharpness
At the crest of Philolaos.
  But, Arabia starting forwards
Bears his master from the danger,
And the haughty giant tottering
Neath his own unwieldly weapon
Falls upon the blood stained centre
Of the direful field of combat.
Then the trembling Leonarchon
Saw Gonsalvo's sable charger
Prancing on Circano's offspring;
Saw it plunging, break the firmness
Of the rugged weight of armour—

Saw the vanquished spirit trampled
Neath the hoof encircling iron.

But, meanwhile the lonely warrior
Wrestled in the storm of combat ;
From the hand of huge Diospur
Darts his forest shaking-javelin,
Wracking thro' the fields of ether—
Tearing down the princely honours
Of the lofty pluméd helmet ,
And the lordly hero bending
Scarce escaped the dread destruction,
Ere Helion darkly frowning
Raised his sheathéd club to battle.

Hark ! a sudden peal of thunder
Thrice resounding o'er the nations
Echoes from the circling towers
Spreading fear and death-like paleness.
Clouds of smoke surround the champion,
Lightnings seem to flash around him,
And the Giant of Sorardo,
Groaning in his dying anguish,
Falls to earth a lifeless ruin.
   Yet Diospur, son of Lara,
Thought to wreak a mighty vengeance,
But again the wondrous warrior
Pours the dreaded shafts of anger,
And he feels the fatal missiles
Enter through his bronzéd armour.

Then an awful fear impelled him,
And he shunned the great Alonzo,
Flying with gigantic swiftness

To the great imperial portal.
  Then the hero bade Arabia
Dart along with arrowy fleetness ;
All the wide arena trembles
As they circle round its barriers.
Yet in vain the speed of terror,
Wildering horrors roll upon him,
And again the crashing thunder
Rises from the godlike stranger.
Dark Diospur's faltering footfalls
Tell of the mysterious power.
Brighter, deadlier, gleams the flashing,
Flaming in the lurid smoke wreaths.
Till the vanquished strength of Fire
Sinks amidst the answering pealing,
Till the half adoring nations,
Lost in long and solemn silence,
See the lone Alonzo, victor
O'er the elements of Nature ;
Hail in him the promised offspring
Of the ever glorious Daystar.

ALONZO.

XVII.

XVII.

ALONZO.

Brightly shone the gay refulgence
Of the sun's meridan splendour,
Brightly beamed the irradiate beauty
Of the Daystar's dazzling glory,
As it blazed upon the armour
Of the great triumphant hero ;
As it gleamed upon the breastplate,
Glittering with the jewelled semblance
Of the realms of Amalyrac.
  Proudly, mid the solemn silence,
Moves along Islanda's ruler,
As his hand with gentle guidance
Bids Arabia bear him onward ;
Bear him onward to the Northward,
Where the lordly Leonarchon
Sits enthroned among his princes.
Deep and solemn was the silence—
Like the stillness of the midnight,
That o'erspread the Coliseum,
As the whole of that assembly
Waited for the longed-for moment,
When their mighty Lord arising,
Should release the stranger champion,
Should command the gathered concourse
To depart in peace and blessing.

But no smile of approbation
Gleamed upon the chief of Empire,
As his frowning glances told them
How his cherished hopes had failed him.
And a stern and dark expression
Lowered o'er his kingly features,
When at length his noble figure
Turned towards the anxious nations.
As he stands, his robes of ermine
Flow around in gorgeous fulness,
And his royal arm extended
Lifts on high the emerald sceptre.

Hark! he speaks. No sound, nor whisper
Breaks upon the sovereign mandate,
As it rises clear and stately
O'er the giant Coliseum.
"People of the first of Empires!
"Ye have seen the mystic challenge,
"Ye have seen the stranger Champion
"Victor o'er the Powers of Nature.
"Unto him the gods have given
"Respite from a swift destruction,
"And their goodness has decreed him,
"Time to seek for pardoning mercy;
"But that time has passed unheeded,
"Still he scorns the holy places,
"Still he boasts with impious triumph
"Of the fate of ruined Xiloc.
"Lo! the Heavens have decreed it,
"And it must be now fulfilléd,
"That a day of wrath approacheth,
"That a day of retribution
"Hangs in clouds of terror o'er him.
"They decree it, and we may not
"War against the thrones of glory:
"Therefore bowing to the Immortals,

" I command thee, great Orontes,
" That thou lead this son of Midnight
" Up the winding stairs of granite,
" To the everlasting Altar,
" And that there his soul be pouréd
" In oblation to the immortals,
" Lest that day of retribution
" Whelm us in its awful sorrow.
" But alas, a deeper shadow
" Dims the crown of Amalyrac.
" For the oracle of Wisdom
" Has pronounced a dread commandment.
" It has seen a taint of evil
" Nestling in the Empire's bosom ;
" And the bud that we have cherished,
" Opes a deadly poisoning flower.
" It decrees that Amarantha
" Dwell within the solemn temple
" Of the nation-guarding Wargod.
" There to join the virgin daughters
" Who perform the sacred office ;
" There to tend the rites ordainéd
" By the triumph giving Godhead.
" Amarantha ! I resign thee
" To the Heaven anointed Hierarch ;
" He will guide thee by his counsels,
" He will teach thee with his wisdom,
" Till again the Powers of Glory
" Own the child of Philolaos."

Here he ceased, but half unwilling,
For his secret soul insatiate,
Longed to gain another victim,
Longed to bid the dark Armoura
Seize the High Priest of the Unknown.'
But he dared not : for the people

Loved the venerable Pontiff,
And he knew that none would venture
E'en to touch the sacred garments.

But a sullen, restless movement
Stole around the seats of marble,
Half suppressed groans and whispers
Told the mind of the assembly,
As they heard their haughty Monarch
Careless of the words of ages,
Give Alonzo to destruction.
But it rose in hoarser murmur,
As the people, all impatient,
As the nations scarce restrainéd,
Listened to his treacherous language,
To his subtly woven pretexts,
Wrought to screen his thirst for Empire ;
As they heard their matchless Princess
Dooméd to the Pontiff's power—
To the power of the Hierarch,
Of the carnage-loving Wargod.

And Alonzo wondered deeply,
When the princely Leonarchon,
Bid Orontes', ruler, lead him
To the bloody place of slaughter ;
But he staid his sable charger,
Bending forward with amazement,
As he heard the cruel fortune
Of his beauteous Amarantha.
And though now the carborne Oro,
Leaping from his brazen chariot,
Waving round his gleaming javelin,
Orders on his troops to seize him ;
Though his followers rush upon him

Yet he recks not of his danger,
Knows not of the rising tempest.
For he sees the Wargod's Pontiff
Hastening to enthrall his victim :
Sees her gentle hands outstretchéd ;
Hears her feeble cry for succour,
Views the priest with ghastly triumph,
Drag her from the throne of ivory—
Sees her fall in fainting terror.

Then he rose all wild with fury,
Maddened with his loved one's danger :
Onward darts the black Arabia,
Charging through the hostile legions.
But how shall the Lord of Island
Aid the Star of Amalyrac !
How without some faithful weapon,
Hope to save the weeping Princess ?
All unarmed against a thousand,
One amongst a host of warriors.
Vain his eye, with lightning swiftness,
Seeks the glance of friendly visage,
But he views a sunlike radiance
Shining on the ancient altar ;
Sees the diamond hilted sabre
Beam beside the crown of Empire.

Not a moment does he linger,
Plunging through opposing masses—
Dashing on through ranks arrangéd ;
See the Prince of wide Orontes
Hastes to gain his brazen chariot,
E'en the troops behind the altar,
Filled with superstition, tremble ;
As he comes, their steely arrows
Rattle on his golden armour.
But he stays the black Arabia—
Standing by the ancient altar—

And the amazed people see him
Bending to its graven summit,
Raise unawed the polished splendour
Of the sacred sword Phlegathron.

All was still—the tumult ceaséd—
All that great assembly trembled,
For they thought they felt the presence
Of a more than mortal power,
And Alonzo stood reveaĺéd,
As the Offspring of the Daystar.
    Then the Master of the Eagle
Dropt in fear the emerald sceptre ;
Then the High Priest of the Daystar
Felt a chilly cold run through him :
But the mighty sovereign Pontiff
Slowly rose in calm composure ;
From his venerable visage
Seemed to gleam prophetic fire,
As he thus addressed the people.

"Lo ! the Times before appointed,
"Hasten on to their fulfilment.
"Lo ! the solemn day approacheth,
"When the earth in bending reverence
"Shall obey the Daystar's Offspring.
"For behold he stands before us,
"See he wields the mystic falchion,
"And the shade of dark ambition
"Now must fade before his glory."
Other words and times prophetic,
Had the agéd man reveaĺéd,
But as oft a spark of fire,
Falling on the parchéd herbage,
Wraps the far extended prairie
In one quenchless conflagration—

So the sons of Amalyrac,
Long enduring, slow to vengeance,
When they saw the great Alonzo
Lift on high the bright Phlegathron,—
When they heard the ancient Pontiff
Tell them of the time fulfilléd—
When they saw their weeping Princess
Dragged away to caves and darkness—
Could no more restrain their anger,
Broke the chains of long allegiance,
Burst the bondage of subjection,
Till the giant turrets trembling,
Answered back their curbless fury.
  Fearless shouts for Amarantha,
Haughty cries for Leonarchon,
Echo to the vaults of heaven ;
Tumult, rage, and wild disorder
Rise in louder, louder thunder ;
All along the marble columns
Throngs the crush of crowding nations,
Shrieks of women, groans of dying,
As the multitudes press on them :
Words of wrath and iron vengeance ;
Curses on the cruel Hierarch,
Menaces against the Monarch ;
Deadly combat, shouts of triumph,
Mighty war-cries, jarring music,
Whirled in one terrific chaos,
Startled all the astonished city.
Woe to him whose venturous boldness
Dares to check the people's anger :
Rich adornments, marble fragments,
Broken balustrades and benches,
Ivory footstools, shattered statues—
All that rage could seize for weapons,
Showered upon Orontes warriors,

As they strove to stay the uproar.

Epidaurus, then arousing,
Led by her chivalrous hero,
Rushed to save the Empire's jewel.
High the dark blue banner waveth,
Studded with the stars of silver,
With the azure wingéd symbol,
And tumultuous shouts ascending,
Hail the bird of Philolaos.

Then the heir of wild Ancyra,
Leaping from his place of honor,
Drew his whitely flashing falchion,
And impetuous cut a pathway
Through the arméd troops of Oro;
Till he reached the Eagle standard,
For he sought to hurl it broken,
Tattered on the red arena.
Wildly raged the gathering combat
'Neath its gorgeous folds of purple :
There the chieftain of Phoceia
Hastes to aid his master's legions ;
By him moves the valorous ruler
Of the plains of Agrigano ;
He, the noblest and the bravest
Of the sons of Southern Empire :
He, the first in every danger,
Foremost in the din of battle.
Here Armoura's frowning tyrant,
Flies upon the young Ancyra ;
Araxeia's king advances,
Acrolara's stately ruler,
But the famed Epiromenes
Toils to aid the youthful warrior,
While the veterans of his army,
Sternly battle for their Princess.

Where art thou, O! boastful Oro?
Where is now thy vaunted valor?
Is it thou, who, shrinking, flying,
Seek'st the rear of ranks for shelter?
See the miscreant, pale and trembling,
Dead to honor, dead to glory;
Careless of his sovereign's favor,
Hides him from the storm of battle.
   Ah! how different, how heroic,
Were thy deeds, O! chief of Deiro!
As thou cleftst a bloody pathway
To the heart of Epidaurus;
As thou ledst thy helmèd phalanx
Down into the depths of tumult.

But the upper ranks of people,
Gaze in wonder on the actions
Of the Lord of Island's armies.
   Little recked the victor Champion
Of the deed that he performèd,
When his arm exulting raisèd,
High in air the bright Phlegathron.
Scarce he heard the Pontiff's language,
Scarce awaits till he has ended;
On again Arabia bears him
Through the wrack of rising tumult.
   Vainly did Eurota's Monarch
Seek to bar his ardent progress,
He has felt the maiden sharpness
Of the Daystar's diamond falchion.

High above the girdling barrier,
Bounds the charger of Gonsalvo.
Cleopatra and her daughters—
All the beauty of the Empire,
Starting from their thrones affrighted,

Crowd the circling halls of marble.
Swift he comes, his fiery glances
Quench the hope of sparing mercy.
Swift he comes, the hated Hierarch,
Filled with fury leaves his victim:
Wide his clenchéd hands are stretchéd,
As he utters imprecations—
As his dark distorted features,
Swelled with wrath and hideous anger,
Glare in rage upon Alonzo.
Ha! he grasps the knife of slaughter;
Down it plunges, bright with sharpness,
Dashed at Amarantha's bosom;
But the Heavens forbade the slaughter,
And decreed a sudden vengeance;
For the sword has woke to battle,
Rousing from the sleep of ages,
And its second work of judgment
Lays the heavy headless body,
Bleeding on the polished pavement.

Then the noble chief descending,
Leaves awhile the black Arabia,—
As he springs, his golden armour
Rings upon the varied marble.
  Bending down, the anxious hero
Gently lifts the lovely Princess,
Fondly bears her fainting figure,
Light as crystal snow in winter,
Bears her up the stairs of granite.
Sad behind him, pale and mournful,
Moves the Queen of Epidaurus.
For no danger,—not the greatest,
Could divide her from her daughter;
Nought dissolve the tender union
Of a mother's deep affection.

Now he gains the graven platform,
Where the High Priest of the Unknown
Rests amidst the sacred college ;
And he gives his Amarantha
To their holy—sure protection.
For he knew an ancient reverence
Hung around the sacred office :
Knew that none had aye adventured
To assail the robéd presence
Of the consecrated priesthood.
Slow the sable circle closing,
Shadows round the snow-white figure
Clasped upon her royal mother,
And their silent ranks have veiled her
From the eyes of her Alonzo.

Then the hero, all impatient,
Hastens to regain his charger,
For he views Epiromenes
Struggling with the troops of Oro :
Sees Ancyra's youthful valor
Vainly warring with Armoura ;
Sees how few the sons of Freedom,
Ranged beneath the starry standard,
And he thirsts to aid the contest,
Fearless of the steely barrier,
Stretched in serried ranks between them.

But how oft the life of mortals
Hangs upon the passing moment :
Then Alonzo, Death unshrouded,
Glided nigh thy lonely pathway !
For the Daystar's vengeful Pontiff,
Following stealthily and noiseless,
Seeks to thrust his deadly poignard,
Deep betwixt the plates of armour.

See! how he, with ghastly smiling,
Gazes on his certain victim,
See! how his deceitful weapon
Glances 'neath the imperial helmet:
In a moment it had entered,
And the hope of nations fallen,
But he sees the shade and starting—
Sudden turning, checks the slaughter.
   Then the unholy man beholding,
Groaning for his blighted triumph,
Sprang with rage impurpled visage,
Like a viper on Alonzo.
"Take the vengeance poured by Heaven,"
Shrieked aloud the frantic High Priest,
As he madly dashed his poignard
Through the richly jewelled breastplate.
   But though from Islanda's leader,
Gushed the gory stream of crimson,
Still the blow had spent its fury
Ere it reached his fenceless bosom;
Scarce he felt it—ere he wrenched it
From the thickly plated cuirass;
Ere he drove its rugged bluntness
Deep into the Pontiff's forehead.
"Lie thou there, thou son of darkness,"
Cried the wrong-avenging hero.
"Lie thou there a dread memorial
"Of the righteous wrath of Heaven."

Now again he mounts Arabia,
Now again he leaps the barrier,
Now again the keen Phlegathron
Flames a firebrand o'er his helmet.
Round him spread disordered legions,
Round him rings the clash of armour,
Round him crush the thronging numbers

Of the troops of wide Orontes :
All in vain her valorous princes
Seek to bar the threatening progress,
See they fall beneath the terrors
Of the Daystar's sacred falchion.
  O'er Islanda's kingly ruler
Hung a veil of superstition,
And the sons of Amalyrac
Shrank unwilling from his pathway.
On he burst through ranks opposing ;
Through the legions of Chrynella ;
Through the hardy troops of Xantha—
To the throbbing depth of tumult,
Where the dove af Philolaos,
Where the bird of Leonarchon,
Tangled with their hostile pinions,
Seem to wrestle for the Empire.

But the noble lord of Deiro
Saw Alonzo unrestrainéd,
Dashing towards the imperial standard ;
Swift he sprang to meet the hero—
Curbed Arabia in his prancing—
Wards the sharpness of Phlegathron
With his buckler's silver borders ;
And his skillful hand upraised,
Threatens with his ponderous war-axe.
Long endured the doubtful combat,
Long the chieftain's desperate courage
Battled fiercely with Alonzo ;
· But at length the mystic sabre
Enters through the plates of silver,
And the sorrowing sons of Deiro
Bear away their wounded Monarch,
Crimson'd with the flowing life blood.

But the victor sees Ancyra
Sinking 'neath Armoura's power:
Low in dust is laid the helmet
Of the sovereign of Phoceia;
And the young and dauntless hero,
Grateful hailed Alonzo's succour,
As he saw the frowning tyrant,
Groaning, sent to realms of Midnight.

Now at length, Epiromenes,
Toiling through the troops of Oro,
Brought to bay her coward Monarch.
Then was tried the boaster's prowess,
Then was shown his vaunted valour,
Down he knelt and prayed for mercy,—
Trembling craved for lengthened life-time,
Told of dark and hidden secrets,
Known to him alone of mortals;
Told of death and dark devices,
That he would reveal hereafter.
Scornfully the stately leader
Listened to the cringing monarch,
Scornfully he gazed upon him,
As he bade his warriors bind him.
    Then he turns again to battle,
Turns again to direful combat,
As he sees the great Alonzo,
Warring 'neath the imperial standard,
Warring with the sturdy boldness
Of the Lord of Agrigano;
Of the chief who bears the banner
Of the princely Leonarchon.

But the golden Eagle trembles,
Agrigano falters forward,
Staggers backward, sinking slowly,

For his glazing eyes no longer
See the cheering light of Heaven,
And his powerless arm refuses
To sustain his master's ensign ;
For Phlegathron's edge has entered
To the source of life and being,
And his soul has joined the spirits
Of departed chiefs and heroes.

Then the gorgeous eagle falling
Sunk upon the red arena,
And its silken folds were tattered,
Trampled 'neath the arméd warriors.
Then Alonzo raised the banner
Of the glorious Philolaos,
Waved it high above the arena,
As he led the joyous legion
Of the queenly Epidaurus.
Onward dashed Epiromenes,
Spreading fear around his pathway,
Onward sprang the young Ancyra,
Darting on the hostile Phalanx.
Amarantha ! Amarantha !
Swelled above the mighty tumult ;
Amarantha ! Amarantha !
Answered back the dark red towers,
As the exulting sons of Empire
Saw the hero lead the battle.

Thus the King of Amalyrac
Saw amazéd all his bravest—
Noblest princes fall around him,
Saw the doom of impious Hierarchs,
Saw the treacherous deeds of Oro,
Saw his own imperial standard

Bow before the deep blue banner,
And his haughty spirit rising,
Could no longer rest inglorious.
Stern he left the throne of ages,
Casting off the robes of ermine ;
Drew his gold emblazoned falchion,
And majestic in his ardour,
Strode to stay the gathering evil.

But the people on the turrets,
On the topmost tiers of marble,
Gazed no more upon the conflict ;
For a solemn sound of thunder
Boomed afar o'er hill and valley,
And before their wondering eyesight
Towered a fleet of lofty vessels ;
High upon the foremost, glittering
In the dazzling beams of summer,
Danced the lions, flamed the dragon,
Soared the sombre pinioned raven :
Clouds of smoke enwreathed their canvas
As their giant forms approaching
Swept across the troubled water.
Hark ! again the pealing thunder
Bursts upon the trembling city.
Tall upon his arrowy vessel
Rose Gonsalvo's lordly figure
Crowned again with victor laurels :
For the bounteous hand of Heaven
Had descended rich with favours,
And had veiled the night of Pylos
In the rainbow beams of triumph.

O ! how welcome was the morning
To the deep desponding Islesmen,

As it streamed upon the beauties
Of the flowery banked Eurotas ;
  Yet a vision still more cheering
Shed a brighter joy around them,
As they saw a friendly squadron
Gliding up the spreading river,
As they saw Cruzatlan's ensign
Waving o'er the tall bananas.

Then the coming day of glory
Dawned upon the sorrowing Islesmen,
And the sun of Hope illumined
All Islanda's blazoned pennons,
As again Gonsalvo led them
Up the fair translucent river.

Who shall tell the midnight conflict
On the beetling steeps of Pylos !
Muffled oars, unbroken silence,
Landing troops, assailing legions !
Who shall tell the unequalled dangers
Of the slippery rocks of granite ;
Tell how suddenly her armies
Started at the warrior shadows
Gathering on her topmost bulwarks—
Saw the landward portals opened,
Heard the war-cry of Zorayda—
Felt the vengeful sword of Ardoc,
Till the banner of Islanda
Floated proudly o'er her towers ;
Till the fleets in festive order
Swept beneath her misty forehead,
And the rising sun beheld them
Move in triumph and rejoicing
O'er the clear pelucid water
Of the lake of Amalyrac.

Thus the nations wondering see them
Bearing down upon the city,
Darkly shading o'er the archways
Of the ancient granite causeway ;
See the throng of crowding people
Hail with shouts the stately squadron,
See the guardians of the city
March to stay their hostile entrance.

All around the iron drawbridge
Raged the roar of civil battle ;
Shouts and screams and dashing water,
Boom of cannon, ring of armour :
Here the legions of the Monarch
Strive to close the widening passage,
Here the people, bold, determined,
Seek to force a broader opening,
Till a deafening cry ascending,
Tells the ending of the struggle ;
Till the sable fleets majestic,
One by one in silent grandeur,
Enter through the spacious drawbridge—
Enter the imperial city.

Then the lordly sons of Island,
Landing 'neath the impending shadow
Of the mighty Coliseum—
Prancing on their stately chargers—
Rangèd round the dark blue banner,
Pass before the awe-struck people.
Now they wind the gradual steepness
Of the capitolian roadway—
As the great Gonsalvo leads them
To the vast imperial portal.
O ! that hour had well repaid him
For his long enduring troubles ;
For he heard Alonzo movèd

Still among the sons of mortals ;
And his thankful eyes upraiséd,
Owned the mighty power of Heaven
That in goodness had decreed him
Thus to see his wish accomplished ;
Had decreed the time of parting,
Time of sorrow should be ended,
And that he again rejoicing,
Should behold his godlike brother.

But as oft the howling tempest,
Stirring up the ocean's billows,—
Dashing wild their foaming whiteness,
Sudden sinks in breathless silence ;
So the thundering roar arising
From the tumult shaken towers—
From the crowded Coliseum,
Died away in funeral stillness,
And a voiceless calm succeeded.
To that jarring clang of discord.

Lo ! the striving sons of Empire
Slow retiring leave the centre—
Slow retiring cease the conflict—
For a mighty chief has fallen,
Fallen from his thronéd grandeur ;
For the offspring of Almodad,
Motionless and pale as marble,
Lies outstretched upon the arena.

Solemn, deep, and awe-struck reverence
Spread its pinions o'er the nations ;
For they felt a kingly spirit
Had departed from their borders,
And though hatred and rebellion

Rose against his dark ambition;
Yet the people in the stillness
Of that aye remembered moment,
Half forgot the days of sorrow,
All the mourning he had brought them,
As they gazed upon the figure
Of the fallen Leonarchon.

There he lay, his noble forehead
Glittered with the high tiara,
By his side the broken falchion—
In his breast the deadly javelin
That had closed the scene of combat.
None had viewed the hand that ventured
To assail the imperial presence,
None e'er knew whose eye unerring,
Aimed the messenger of vengeance.
There he lay, the haughty Monarch,
Pale and dead among his people;
Pale and dead—no tear of sorrow
Dewed the urn of Lamentation
For the soul of the departed.
  There he lay, a solemn warning
Of the end of dark ambition,
Of the gloomy end of striving
To enthrone a Tyrant Empire
On the ancient seat of Freedom.

But the Priests around the altar,
Moving on in sable order,
Spread the tattered eagle banner
O'er the form of the departed.

Then the great victorious Champion,
Bearing the unconquered ensign

Of the House of Philolaos,
Guides Arabia to the altar;
And his kingly voice arising,
Spake unto the assembled concourse :

" Nations of the first of kingdoms !
" People of the Daystar's city !
" Pale in death upon the arena,
" Lies Almodad's regal offspring :
" Leonarchon's hand no longer
" Holds the sacred reins of power.
" Therefore I demand the Empire—
" Claim the throne of Amalyrac
" For the House of Philolaos ;
" Claim the gleaming diamond circlet
" For the Princess Amarantha."

Then from all the answering nations,
Thundered forth their loud rejoicing ;
Then the starry standard waved
From the Coliseum's towers.
But the lovely Amarantha,
Rising from her fainting terrors,
Heard amazed the Lord of Island,
Claim for her the diamond circlet :
And she thought she still was dreaming,
As the venerable Pontiff
Led her down the stairs of granite—
Down unto the ancient altar.
Deeply did she love Alonzo,
Proud of all his deeds of valour,
And though, when she heard her hero
Tell the toils that he had mastered,
She had wondered at his prowess :
Yet as now herself beheld him,

Warring with superior dangers—
Victor in the deadliest combats—
Deeper admiration filled her;
And she too had hailed her champion
As the offspring of the Daystar.

But meanwhile the troops of Island
Pass along the imperial city:
Pass beneath the giant vastness
Of the dark red Coliseum:
Gaze upon the dizzy archway—
On the frowning southern portal.
Eagerly Gonsalvo leading
Hastens 'neath the sombre shadow;
And his darting eye astonished
Views the silent throng of nations,
Sees the wide arena stainéd
With the wreck of recent battle;
Broken armour, shattered fragments,
Fallen warriors, slaughtered giants,
And among them, huge and shapeless,
Monster sons of former nature.

In the centre, 'neath the covering
Of a shivered, tattered banner,
Lay the javelin piercéd body
Of some great departed hero.
He had thought it was Alonzo,
But he saw no Monarch seated
Midst the princes of the nations;
Saw a black and fiery charger
Prancing 'neath a stately warrior,
Who empanoplied in armour,
Bearing high a starry standard,
Rode along the Northern bulwark

Of the barrier circled precincts,
And at once his lightning glances
Knew the form of his Arabia.
And the welcome truth embraced him,
That at length his godlike brother
Stood again before his vision.

Then his ardent joy had led him
O'er the place of recent combat—
Led him instant o'er the arena
To the side of the Dictator.
But he sees a dark robed systrum
Ranged beneath the throne of ivory,
Sees a reverend man descending
Lead a snow-white form of beauty
Down the sovereign trodden staircase—
Down unto the ancient altar.

O'er his venerable forehead
Shone a gold enwreathed serpent
On its scaly crest upraised
Glowed a glittering star of sapphire;
Round her youthful brows encircling,
Beamed a gem enriched tiara;
But a veil of broidered tissue
Hid her features from the hero.

Then the venerable Pontiff
Raised his holy hands in blessing;
And his voice in tones melodious,
Filled the crowded Coliseum.

" Blessèd be the solemn hour
"Of the times before appointed !
" Happy are the favored people

"Who behold the days prophetic;
"Who behold the words fulfilléd,
"Graven on the golden altar.
"For dark ages rolling onward,
"Bring the circling cycles round us,
"And the footsteps of the seasons
"Have attained the mystic number;
"For the offspring of the Daystar,
"Armed with thunder, armed with lightning—
"Moving swifter than the Eagle—
"Fiercer than the raging Lion,
"Has required his father's kingdom.
"Amalyrac, thou has trembled,
"And thy mighty king has fallen—
"All the words have been accomplished;
"And the daily sacrifices,
"And the mystical processions
"Winding up the sacred temple,
"Have for ever—ever ceaséd.
"Glorious truths of highest Heaven
"Shall be now revealed to you;
"And the veil of times prophetic
"Be removéd from before you;
"Till the hidden words emblazoned
"In the Holiest of Holies,—
"Till the mystery of the Daystar
"Burst in light celestial on you—
"Till ye know the Powers immortal
"Love not blood of slaughtered victims,
"Till ye learn no more to worship
"At the altars of the Midnight,—
"Till ye turn away in horror
"From the carnage-loving Wargod.

"Lo! the Heavens have poured their bles-
        sings

"On the child of Philolaos;
"They have given to her a guardian,
"Nearer, dearer than her father,
"And the Offspring of the Daystar
"Has required for her the kingdom.
"He requires it; he demands it;
"And we must obey the mandate.
"Lo! we give the diadem to her;
"Give to her the emerald sceptre,
"Give to her to be enthroned
"O'er the realms of Amalyrac:
"And we hail Thee as our Sovereign—
"As our Empress, Amarantha!"

Ere he ceased the aged Pontiff,
Bending slowly o'er the altar,
Raised the ancient diamond circlet
High above its sacred cornice;
And enthroned its beaming radiance
On the gently blushing forehead
Of the Rose of Amalyrac.

Then the veil of broidered tissue
Hid no more her queenly beauty:
Then Gonsalvo, lost in wonder,
Gazed upon her perfect features;
Then the princes and the nations,
Filled with ecstasy and rapture,
Hailed the child of Philolaos.
Till the myriads of her people
Raised their choral exultation
Far along the mighty city.
While above them blazed the glories
Of the everlasting Daystar.

CHORUS.

Long live the Empress, the peerless in beauty !
Long may she flourish ! Long may she prosper !
Long may the diadem'd pride of the Empire
Beam on the brows of the bright Amarantha.

Hail to the Empress ! beloved by her people !
Hail to the Hero ! the son of the Daystar !
Long may the Amaranth, twined in a garland
Wreathe the tall form of the Lord of Phlegathron.

Hail ! to the Heaven-born days that are coming,
The orient splendour of ages of Freedom,
Bursting in all their radiant refulgence
O'er the wide realms of the first of the Kingdoms.

Hail to the hour, whose hallowéd presence
Ends the long line of the mournful procession,
Ends the red stream of slaughter and sorrow,
Poured from the heights of the Altar of Darkness.

Hail to the Standard, the Emblem of Mercy !
The far spreading pinions arising to Glory.
Long may they soar in the pathway of triumph,
Blest by the sons of the High Amalyrac.

THE EMPIRE.

XVIII.

XVIII.

THE EMPIRE.

Who shall tell the joyous meeting
Of the two victorious brothers;
Who the shouts of acclamation
Rising round Islanda's heroes.
Who shall tell the sounds of triumph
Echoing from the domes of Lola,
When the great united army
Heard that Amarantha reignéd;
Who the shade of deep despondence
Cast upon the Empire's leaders,
When they knew that Leonarchon
Rested with departed monarchs—
Knew their sovereign's deed of darkness,
Whispered by the base Orontes;
Who the terror that o'erspread them,
When they saw the golden splendour
Of the Guards of Amalyrac,
Raising proud the starry standard,
Leave the camp, and join the forces—
Join the armies of the Empress;
Tell the mournful day of slaughter,
When the brave Araxes warréd
With Dahcotan's daring leader;
Tell the deeds of the young heroes,
Worthy of Almodad's offspring:
Tell the tears of Cleopatra,

When she heard her son had fallen,
When she heard the noble Theron
Slept the sleep of countless ages;
When she heard her loved Araxes
Fled an exile to the palace
Of Alloria's haughty Monarch.

But the Powers above beholding
Looked in mercy on her sorrow;
When they gave a son to soothe her—
Gave to her a greater offspring—
When Alonso's stately brother
Led Chrysothemis the lovely
To the lofty tower'd portal,
To the gleaming golden altar.

Who shall tell the classic splendour
Of the pompous day of triumph,
When the generous sons of Ardoc
Hail'd the reign of Amarantha?
When they bore the starry standard
Thro' the streets of Amalyrac;
When the famed Epiromenes
Led the Kings of far Orontes;
When Ancyra, midst his princes,
Moved the Monarch of Phoccia;
When the sovereigns of the kingdoms
Swept along in regal order;
And the lordly Amphilonin
Tower'd amidst Dahcotan's warriors—
Rode amidst the imperial greatness
Of the realms of fair Xilocan;
When the High Priest of the Unknown—
Ever honour'd by the nation—
Second father to the Empress,
Led the long and grand procession

Up the solemn Via Sacra,—
Up the ancient graven staircase,—
'Neath the heaven aspiring towers,—
'Neath the domes of vaulted granite,—
All along the aisléd vastness
Of the consecrated precincts,
To the Holiest of Holies.
When the whole united empires
Filled with joy and exultation,
Saw the Amaranth wreathe its flowers
Round the Offspring of the Daystar.

Who shall tell the wondrous story
Of the glory of the kingdom :
How again the sun of Freedom
Gilded all the fanes of Mora ;
How Alloria poured his armies
In the cause of young Araxes ;
How the fertile plains of Cona—
All the sources of Orontes
Bowed before the great Alonzo,
Till the swelling waves of Empire
Dashed around on subject mountains.

How the sons of wealthy Aclan
Saw the gathering fleets and legions
Leave the waters of Eurotas ;
How the long and desperate combat
Raged beneath Zorayda's towers,
Till the double headed Eagle
Quailed before the dark blue Lions,
Till the starry flag triumphant,
Waved o'er Eleorada's valleys,
And her verdure crownéd islands
Hailed with smiles their lovely Empress.

But the splendour of the Empire
Flows around in fuller radiance,
And its blazing beams redundant
Pour in dazzling brightness round me.
Dim I see its growing grandeur
Fill the gazing world with wonder—
See the fall of dark Mediro—
See the mighty western kingdoms
Fade before the Sun's resplendence.

Till at length Alloria's greatness
Sinks before the Daystar's Offspring ;
Till at length the giant Empire
Sleeps beneath the shadowing olive,
And its branches dewed with freedom,
Spread luxuriant to the ocean.
From the borders of the river,—
From the borders of Eurotas
To the long resounding circuit
Of the ever rolling azure ;
All the nations, all the people,
All her joyous sons and daughters,
Joined in one united chorus.—
One united song of blessing,
As ·they hailed the orient glories
Of the child of Philolaos.

O ! that every favored Kingdom
Had a ruler like Alonzo ;
O ! that every dauntless Hero
Had a brother like Gonsalvo ;
O ! that every earthly Empire
Had an Empress Amarantha.

CONCLUSION.

But the wondrous vision ceaseth;
All the scenes of beauty vanish;
Rolling clouds have spread their darkness
O'er the Eden smiling prospect,
O'er the long majestic outline
Of the mighty southern mountains,
O'er the wide extending champaign
Of the realms of Amalyrac,
O'er the forest hills of Ardoc,
O'er the ancient fanes Xiloc,
O'er the myriad piles of marble
Gleaming round the lake of sapphire,—
Gleaming 'neath the solemn grandeur
Of the Temple of the Daystar.

All has ceased, and nought remaineth,
Nought remains but dear remembrance,
Nought remains but silent wonder
At the mighty power of Fancy.